CORPSE DE BALLET

ALISON STONE

Treehaven Press

Copyright © 2022 by Alison Stone

All rights reserved.

No part of this book may be reproduced in any form or by any electronic or mechanical means, including information storage and retrieval systems, without written permission from the author, except for the use of brief quotations in a book review.

Rev. C

❧ Created with Vellum

CHAPTER ONE

Jayne Murphy hoisted her purple suitcase out of the trunk. It landed with a clack on its plastic wheels. *Darn, it's heavy.* Wind gusted from the north and she grabbed one side of her unbuttoned coat. *Ugh...* Snow and cold were meant for Christmas and Santa's arrival, but once January arrived, it could all melt as far as Jayne was concerned. But not in Tranquility—a suburb of Buffalo—where the potential for cold and snow easily stretched into March—or even April, if Mother Nature was feeling particularly ornery. The month of May might see some flakes if she was truly ticked-off.

Miss Natalie, Jayne's mother, stood with her arms tightly crossed over her thin frame, staring at nothing in particular. She looked lost, more confused than usual. Not for the first time, Jayne wondered if her mother was up for the busy-ness that was a three-day dance competition weekend. They were draining under the best of circumstances. However, it would have broken Jayne's heart to leave her mother—the owner of Murphy's Dance Academy—behind because it was in the world of dance that she showed some of that old, familiar spark. And Jayne feared with each passing day that light might eventually be extinguished.

Jayne slammed the trunk and her mother's blue eyes snapped up to meet hers. Miss Natalie smiled tentatively, the lost look in her eyes suggesting she was struggling for something appropriate to say. Slowly, Alzheimer's was stripping away even the smallest of interactions between mother and daughter.

And so much more than that.

"All set?" Miss Natalie asked with an odd mix of enthusiasm and hesitation that was becoming all too familiar. Before Jayne had a chance to answer, the older woman's pale eyebrow drew down, as if trying to place herself in this almost-empty tundra of a parking lot in Niagara Falls. "Are we going to a party? Is this a party?" Her weary gaze traveled to the nondescript building across the parking lot.

"We're going to a dance competition," Jayne said kindly. A gust of wind whipped a swirl of snowflakes into a mini tornado. Ah, what she wouldn't have done to stay home on this particular Friday afternoon with her toes tucked up under a fleece blanket, watching one of the top ten movies on Netflix. If Jayne could rewind the clock a bit, she might have even invited Danny to the house. There was nothing better than snuggling against his solid chest with his arm around her while they watched mindless TV. However, they had grown distant—his doing, maybe hers, depending on who you asked. His natural sense of protectiveness had begun to interfere with her budding career as a private investigator. As the youngest of four—and the only girl—Jayne had had her share of males trying to tell her what to do under the guise of making sure she was safe.

And she was tired of it.

PI work was her livelihood. Her passion. Not her role as administrator at her mother's dance studio—as important as that was for her mother's wellbeing. No, she planned to build her career working under Teddy at Wysocki and Sons' Investigations to get the requisite training to become a licensed private investigator in the great state of New York. Some might say it was her sloppy seconds of a career since her dream from the time she was a little girl was to be a Tranquility police officer. A dream that had come to a screeching halt due to family obligations.

Shoving the thoughts aside, she adjusted the strap of the oversized tote on her shoulder and grabbed the handle of the beast of a rolling suitcase. She wished she had an extra hand to urge her mother along since her gait had gotten slow as of late and Jayne feared she'd misstep and fall. The same woman who was still graceful in the dance studio. *The mind and body are fascinating things.*

"Let's get out of the cold, Miss Natalie." Her mother seemed most responsive to the name her dance students had called her for over forty years. "We'll check into our hotel room." Even though Niagara Falls was only a short drive from Tranquility, staying on-site made the late nights and early mornings of the dance competition a lot easier.

Miss Natalie nodded. "Sounds good. Then perhaps we can get some tea."

"It's a plan."

The women entered the lobby of the hotel that was connected to the convention center, the location of Superstar Dance Power competition. The lobby was empty, as most of the dance teams would be arriving in a couple hours. Jayne had wanted to avoid the crowds as much as she could because they tended to agitate her mother.

They checked in, then took the elevator to the fourteenth floor—high enough to see the spray of the falls, but not the falls themselves. A person had to go about a block southeast and spend a couple hundred dollars more per night to score that view, even in the dead of winter. Jayne dropped the tote on the bed closest to the door and hoisted the ungainly suitcase onto the stand and unzipped it. Out of the corner of her eye, she noticed her mother standing still. Jayne straightened and smiled, her heart breaking for her beautiful mother who seemed to be waiting for instructions in the unfamiliar space.

"Are we late?" Miss Natalie glanced down at her watch, but Jayne suspected her mother had forgotten how to tell time, or more likely, lost the ability to measure it. Jayne hated that she was constantly taking stock of her mother's symptoms, trying to see where on the slippery slope of Alzheimer's she was currently positioned. The assessment was made more difficult because each day—and time of day— was different.

Stop! Focus on the now!

"No, we're perfectly on time." Jayne pulled back the heavy curtains. Any mist from the falls blended with the rapidly falling snow. Unsurprisingly, the competition hadn't been canceled—such was life when you lived in a locale where it snowed a lot. If they canceled an event every time a storm was forecasted—and they didn't always get it right—they'd never do anything between November and March besides hunker down at home with a good book. Not that Jayne would mind.

"Do we need to be somewhere?" Despite Jayne's best efforts, her mother continued to press, her growing agitation rubbing off on Jayne.

Jayne guided her mother to a chair. "Not for a little while. Let's unpack first."

While her mother watched, Jayne took the contents of the suitcase and put them in the drawers. It was something her mother had always insisted they do at these events because it made things a little bit easier. The simple act reminded Jayne how excited she used to be to stay at a hotel as a child. Back then, her dance teammates would gather in one of the hotel rooms, freshly showered and in their PJs, giggling and sharing snacks. Then, on Monday, exhausted from a weekend of too much dance and not enough sleep, she'd beg her mother to let her skip school.

Just when she thought her mother was going to cave, her father gave the official "not gonna happen in my house." Her father, a police officer, had always been a task master, albeit a benevolent one. The rule follower in him wouldn't allow his only daughter to skip school. What kind of example would that be? Jayne's heart warmed at the sweet memory of her dad, who had died when she was the tender age of fifteen.

"Mom, want to go to the coffee shop? Unwind a bit before the solo competitions start?" Jayne asked, reminding her mother of their plans.

"Some tea would be wonderful," her mother said.

When they went back down to the lobby, Jayne caught sight of Miss Gigi, the owner of the only other dance studio in Tranquility, standing at the check-in counter with one of her dancers. Not in the mood to engage in idle chit-chat, Jayne tried to hurry her mother along, but it was fruitless. Miss Natalie seemed distracted by the unfamiliar surroundings, especially the flashing lights and electronic sounds from the slot machines in the casino whose entrance was positioned on the far side of the lobby. The flashing lights and *ding-ding-ding* sounds were designed to draw people in, including those who didn't belong. But the security guards would see that they stayed out. Jayne gave one last glance toward check-in and sure as all get out, she regretted it. She and Miss Gigi locked eyes. A zing of betrayal on behalf of her mother shot through her. Gigi had trained at Murphy's Dance Academy since she was three years old, transitioned into a favored teacher, then left to open a competing studio. The ungrateful woman had also tried to poach MDA's dance teachers, but thankfully, they were more loyal than she had been.

Miss Natalie commanded a lot of respect in this industry. As office manager, Jayne prayed she'd be able to maintain the studio's stellar reputation because dance was what gave her ailing mother purpose.

"Come on, Miss Natalie, this way."

Her mother patted Jayne's hand curled around the crook of her elbow. "I don't know what I'd do without you." It was an uncharacteristic moment of self-awareness.

Jayne reached across and patted her mother's hand in return. "The feeling is mutual." She glanced up at the Tim Horton's sign, the words wavy in her watery vision. "I think we should get a donut too."

CHAPTER TWO

The deep thump of a rap song that was popular long before any of these young dancers were alive filled every inch of the cavernous convention center space. Jayne sat down with her mother near the stage on the aisle, away from the mammoth speakers. They had their choice of seats since the weather was delaying most of the attendees.

Miss Natalie sat ramrod straight, staring intently at the empty stage, fingering the delicate fabric of her flowing skirt.

"Nothing like the dance competition vibe. Right, Miss Natalie?" Jayne had been tagging along with her mom to these venues for as long as she could remember.

Her mother nodded slowly and a tremulous smile curved her pale lips. A light sparked in her eyes. This—*this*—was why Jayne took pains to keep her mother involved with the world that had been her life even after her diagnosis.

"Are my dancers going on soon?" Miss Natalie asked. She co-taught with another instructor, and her dancers, many having started dancing as toddlers, loved her like a grandmother.

"Tonight they're running the solos." Even though her mother no longer choreographed those numbers, all the dancers at Murphy's Dance Academy were "her dancers." They were her legacy.

"We should get backstage then." Her mother stood in one graceful move and looked at Jayne. "Shouldn't we go?"

"Yes, for a little bit," Jayne said, forcing a cheerful tone above the loud music. "Then we'll watch from the audience." She found herself scanning the faces in the crowd, praying that soon one would belong to Hannah. Her teen neighbor had a calming way with her mother and Jayne had hired her to hang out with Miss Natalie for the weekend. Jayne paid the teen, but she suspected the girl would do it for free.

Her mother's bright blue eyes traveled the length of her only daughter, apparently taking in her blue jeans and winter boots. "Are you dancing soon? Maybe you should get ready." Her mother's voice sounded frail, distracted, confused, her determination to go backstage forgotten.

"Not today," Jayne said, purposely vague so as not to further disorient her mother. Miss Natalie's disappointment that her only daughter had quit dance at age twelve ran deep and tended to resurface every so often. Jayne's plans to follow her father and brothers into law enforcement made pointe, jazz, tap, and hip-hop unnecessary.

Turns out, all their plans had come crashing down.

"We can see the dancers backstage if you'd like," Jayne said, trying to keep her mother on track.

"Oh, okay." Miss Natalie lifted a shaky hand to her mouth, a gesture Jayne recognized as confusion. She was trying to put things in their proper place.

Jayne led her mother to the stage and around the billowing curtain. She heaved a sigh of relief when she found Paige Wentworth and Cindy Peters doing some standing stretches, bending their leg and pressing their foot to their backside. "Look, there's Paige and Cindy. They have their solos tonight." Jayne added as many cues as she could to keep her mother focused.

Miss Natalie caught sight of two of her seniors, girls she'd known since they wore pink tutus and tiny ballet shoes, and smiled. "Ah, yes." A flicker of recognition—familiarity—brightened her face and eased the knot in Jayne's belly.

Paige noticed them first and nudged her friend. The two young women closed the distance between with graceful movements. "Hi, Miss Natalie, Miss Jayne," they said in unison.

"Did you hear the team from Syracuse didn't make it in because of the snowstorm?" Cindy asked, sounding a little too gleeful. "That means they won't have anyone in the solo, fifteen and up category."

Jayne lifted an eyebrow. "What fun is competition without any real competition?"

"Their studio always wins all the awards," Cindy said. "It's time they give someone else a chance." Jayne suspected the teen was repeating the words of her mother.

"Do your best, that's all we ask." Jayne's gaze drifted over to Paige, who shrugged. Her parents were going through a nasty divorce—thanks in part to Jayne's PI skills with a camera set up on a dark street outside her father's girlfriend's house. It was unlikely the young woman was too worried about which dance studios were or weren't in attendance. Paige seemed almost indifferent to dance, and Jayne had heard through the grapevine that she was hanging with some questionable people.

"Go out and do your best," Miss Natalie said. "The only person you're competing against is yourself."

Jayne smiled. Some lessons ran deep, and even memory

issues couldn't erase them—yet. Jayne leaned close to her mother's ear to speak over the pulsing music. "Let's watch from the audience." She quickly checked her watch. "We don't want to miss the first number."

"It can't start without me." A tall man who was news-broadcaster handsome in an early '70s kind of way—like the men she had seen on some of the crime documentaries from that era— approached them with a wide grin. *Dale Diamond*. His once-white veneers were now slightly yellowed. He took Miss Natalie's hand and brushed a kiss across the back of it. Her mother blushed. "How is my favorite studio owner?" Mr. Diamond asked, straightening. His smile was still in place but close up Jayne could see that it didn't reach his eyes.

Miss Natalie pressed her hand to her chest. "Fine, fine." The warm glow of flattery fell from her face and was replaced with the all-too-familiar vacant look of confusion.

"Hello, Mr. Diamond, it's nice to see you," Jayne said to take the attention away from her mother, and at the same time, give her a cue. "I'm Jayne Murphy, Natalie's daughter." Her cheery tone felt a little bit over the top. It was becoming a habit.

Even though Jayne had only been a child when she first met Mr. Diamond, a flush of embarrassment always reminded her of how cruel children could be. How cruel *she* could be. As a young dancer, Jayne and her teammates had referred to Mr. Diamond as Ron Burgundy behind his back. He was exactly the kind of showman Will Ferrell was mocking in the movie *Anchorman*, and the dancers took tremendous delight in having made the connection, probably because an adult had pointed it out. Even now, his brown hair was a few shades too dark for his wrinkled face. His hard-shell comb-over didn't help, either. The man was known as a flirt in the industry but was devoted to his daughter and his deceased wife.

Stop it.

Ah, to be blessed with a quick wit, only to be weighed down by empathy and a conscience.

"Yes, I remember. Nice to see you again." The look in his eyes suggested he wanted to inquire about her mother's health but wouldn't dare to in front of her. Either that, or something else was weighing on him.

"Is your daughter here today?" Jayne asked, redirecting his curiosity. Lola Diamond was a late-in-life child for the Diamond family, but she had been Dale's last hope for someone to hit it big in the dance world. He had tried to make it in New York. Some had said he was a triple threat talented in dance, singing, and acting. But as the years wore on, he found himself picking up odd jobs as an announcer for dance competitions until Super Star Dance Power had hired him full time, paid him well, and allowed him to travel the country. He hadn't made it as a dancer, but his career ran adjacent to those who still were young enough to dream.

When his only daughter grew into a talented dancer, he beamed with pride when she'd won award after award. Mr. Diamond had the privilege of announcing his daughter's name, but he made a point to remind the audience that he didn't have a say in who won. It had become his shtick.

"Lola's in New York looking to make her name on Broadway." The man with the silky baritone voice shook his head almost imperceptibly. "Such a tough business." Perhaps it pained him even more to see his daughter struggle.

"Oh," Miss Natalie muttered, probably trying to figure out how the little girl who used to dance in the same age group as Jayne's neighbor, Melinda, was now old enough to live on her own in New York. Not a lot of dancers who trained in Buffalo made the trip downstate. Or, if they did, their stay didn't last long.

Mr. Diamond's skin glowed an unnatural shade of beige.

"I look forward to seeing the dancers from Murphy's Dance Academy. Always do. They're top notch." His mouth slanted into a half smile and he leaned slightly closer, as if to share a secret. "I think some of the teams weren't able to make it because of the storm."

"That's unfortunate," Jayne said, hating to think of anyone stranded on the snowy roads. "I hope they're safe and warm."

"Well..." Mr. Diamond pushed back his shoulders and ran a hand (unnecessarily) across his perfectly coiffed hair. "I better kick things off." He turned on shoes so shiny a person could see their reflection in them. He jogged up the metal stairs to the makeshift stage, giving off the energy of a much younger man. Jayne suspected that was his intention. The man's appearance was impeccable. A real showman.

A pretty blonde Jayne didn't recognize stepped out of view a moment before a disembodied hand passed him a mic from behind the curtain. Mr. Diamond strode to the middle of the stage and, as if the spirit of Ron Burgundy had possessed his body, he said in a smooth voice, "Welcome to the Superstar Dance Power Competition at Niagara Falls." The audience erupted into applause. "We have some of the most talented dancers from all over North America here today. Can I have a heck yeah from our Canadian friends?" A rowdy group in the back corner let out a "heck yeah" followed by a "whoop whoop."

Jayne wondered if that team had made the strategic decision to drive in earlier to beat the storm. The convention center seemed to be filling in a bit, promising some competition, at least. She and her mother found their seats and settled in.

Jayne scanned the crowd again, searching for Hannah. As much as she relied on the young woman, she shouldn't make her drive in this weather. Jayne would have to text her and tell her to stay home where she'd be safe and warm.

Jayne's conscience pinged her for not having thought of that earlier. She quickly sent the text before she changed her mind, then leaned back in the metal chair to watch the first dancer gracefully sashay onto the stage.

CHAPTER THREE

Hannah aimed the key fob at her trunk and popped it open with a click and creak. A thin layer of fluffy white snow slid down the lid. The forecast was calling for six to nine inches in the next twenty-four hours, but if she hurried, she should miss the brunt of it. Or so she hoped. She probably should have skipped the after-school bowling club and gone to the dance competition directly with Jayne and Miss Natalie, but Hannah was trying to make more friends her age. Despite being a senior in high school, she had only moved to Tranquility at the beginning of the school year—not exactly the best time to move when you're an awkward kid who'd thought going Goth was the best way to make a good first impression. After meeting Jayne, she had transitioned out of the rebellious stage and back to strawberry blonde and a requisite uniform of Ugg boots, jeans, and a college sweatshirt. Now, she blended in.

Hannah tossed her backpack into the trunk then checked the time on her phone before stuffing it in her coat pocket. *Ugh.* She was running late. Nothing unusual about that. She had promised Jayne she'd meet her in Niagara Falls before the competition started, and she was at least thirty minutes away if she got on the road right now. In good weather. With this snow, all bets were off. She wasn't much of a fan of driving in snow, so she wouldn't be breaking any speed records. So much for promises.

Hannah's phone chimed in her pocket. A text from Jayne: *Don't come. Too snowy.*

Hannah sighed heavily. This was her out, but she really needed the money from this gig for college this fall. She had applied to five schools and was waiting on pins and needles to hear if she got into the last two, one of which was her top choice. She was a little worried about her ACT scores but hoped her essays and stellar grades would put her over the top. Even if Jayne wasn't paying her, she couldn't let her down. Her neighbor relied on her to keep Miss Natalie company. Hannah's gaze drifted to the street in her quiet cut de sac. There was only a dusting of snow. Jayne's text was probably out of an abundance of caution.

Hannah's thumbs hovered over her phone screen, about to compose a text telling Jayne she'd be fine and she was coming anyway, then she decided against it. She didn't want Jayne to insist she not come. Jayne was overly responsible like that. Hannah would pretend she didn't see the text. For all Jayne knew, Hannah was already on the road. They both knew Hannah never checked her phone while driving. After their neighbor Melinda was run off the road, they had all become more conscientious drivers.

Set on her plan, Hannah reached for the car door handle when something in the heavily shadowed yard caught the corner of her eye. The hairs on the back of her neck prickled to life and a flush of goosebumps blanked her skin. A loud crash made her freeze in place, uncertainty clouding her thinking. Should she jump in the car and hightail it out of there? Or should she run back inside her house? A burst of adrenaline had her moving toward the sound, the inch of snow squeaking under her shoe. The sooner she determined it was nothing, the sooner she could leave.

"No," she muttered. *What am I doing?*

The Greens' home next door was empty. They had recently placed it on the market, but according to a conversation she'd overheard between her mother and Mr. Green, they hadn't had too many showings. Apparently, no one wanted to live in the house where a psychotic killer had once lived, even if only when visiting her dad and stepmom. But it wasn't like Carol Anne butchered her family in the living room or anything. Her out-of-control jealousy had caused her to run her stepsister off the road into the river. *That's all.* Hannah shuddered at the callousness of it. How could someone do that?

Hannah let out a sigh. Carol Anne was locked up, under psychiatric evaluation or something before she stood trial. She couldn't hurt anyone now. People would eventually forget about the murderer who once lived on this street. Someone would buy the house. Perhaps once the weather got nicer. No one wanted to move in the dead of winter in the middle of the school year. It was hard enough coming to a new school in September. She knew from experience.

Hannah's gaze drifted to the yard again. Her family's driveway was adjacent to the Greens' with only a thin strip of grass separating them. There was no reason for anyone to be in the backyard. The dark shadows in the swirling snow had apparently made her unnecessarily jittery. She strained to listen, but all she could hear was the clacking of bare tree branches in the wind and some forgotten frantic chimes somewhere in the distance. Man, all those true crime shows filled her head with a lot of worse-case scenarios. She didn't know why she did that to herself. The noise was probably some wind-related property damage. A gutter smashing a window or something.

Hannah glanced at her own dark house. Her parents had gone to visit her grandmother for the weekend. She muttered under her breath. Jayne and Hannah, two of the Greens' neighbors, had promised the grieving couple they'd keep an eye on the house since Mrs. Green had gone for an extended stay with her sister in Florida, and Mr. Green had thrown himself into traveling for business, meeting his wife in Florida when he had the time. The chicken that Hannah was, she didn't want to go back into her own empty house, so she did what any sensible young woman would do—she climbed inside her car, locked the doors, cranked the engine (and the heat) and called the one cop she had in her contacts.

Danny Nolan picked up on the first ring. She adjusted the heat and kept the phone pressed to her ear as she answered Danny's barrage of questions.

Yes, I'm safe.

No, I didn't see anyone.

No, Jayne's not home (and why do you ask?).

"I'm on my way." Danny was the nicest guy. He insisted on staying on the phone with Hannah while he responded to her call. Thankfully, he was on duty, so it wasn't like she was bothering him. This was basically his job, but still, she was grateful for his immediate response.

The rapidly accumulating snow had covered the windshield, creating a cozy cocoon inside her vehicle, but it also obstructed her view of a potential bad guy.

"Can you see anything?" Danny asked.

"Hold on." Hannah twisted the stem on the steering wheel and the motor whined a half-beat before the wiper blades swooshed across the windshield. "A lot of snow."

Another set of headlights arced across the yard. "Someone's here," Hannah said, her voice cracking.

"That's me," Danny said.

"Oh," she laughed nervously. "Okay." She turned the engine off and climbed out, immediately missing the warmth of the heat pumping out of the vents. An arctic wind whipped against her neck and she jerked up her zipper.

Danny had already gotten out of his car and his solid frame was backlit by the lights on his patrol car. He reached out and touched her shoulder. "You okay?"

"Yeah, yeah, just concerned because the Greens are out of town," Hannah said.

As the only daughter of two self-absorbed professionals, Hannah soaked up Danny's attention. She was still trying to figure out her place in this small town. Her new persona had gained her a little traction with her classmates, including a coffee date with a mathlete. (A nice kid, but not her type.)

But Danny... Hannah couldn't understand why Jayne kept finding fault with him. It was like she wanted to sabotage their relationship before it really got going. She totally could relate that Jayne didn't want another cop second-guessing all her decisions, but man, it seemed like a small price to pay when the cop was a good-looking, kind-hearted guy like Danny. But it wasn't like Hannah had the experience to give her neighbor dating advice, unless it involved the main character on a popular show she was streaming on Netflix. And even then, things seemed to get tied up in a neat little bow.

"I was leaving to meet Jayne and Miss Natalie at the dance convention in Niagara Falls and I heard something. Sounded like glass breaking. My neighbors aren't around, so I thought I shouldn't leave." *Even though that's exactly what she wanted to do.* Hannah's gaze tracked up to the house that seemed like a former shell of itself. According to Jayne, the small house used to be aglow with lights when Melinda was still alive. She had been a popular girl with a lot of friends coming and going. Hannah had only moved in a few months before her neighbor's tragic death and hadn't had the chance to know her. Being Goth Girl had set her apart. Regret washed over Hannah. Now it was too late. Now, the least she could do was make sure poor Melinda's parents' house was secure until they sold it. Maybe a young family would move in and make the place come alive again.

Danny touched her arm, snapping her out of her spiraling thoughts. "Stay here while I check it out."

"Okay... Do I...um...have to wait? I'm running late." Hannah didn't relish driving in this weather, and the longer she waited, the worse it might get.

"Please. I'll need to ask you a few more questions." Danny flipped his collar up and disappeared around the back of the house without waiting for her response. Maybe that self-assured cockiness that someone was going to do whatever he said was what had gotten under Jayne's skin. Hannah bounced on the balls of her sneakers, made a mental note to dress warmer, stuffed her hands into her coat pockets, and her fingers brushed across the cool plastic of her cell phone case. She wondered if she should call Jayne but decided against it. She didn't want her good friend to convince her not to come. She was a little too creeped out to stay home alone now.

It felt like an eternity before Danny came back. He must have walked around the entire property. He attempted to stomp the snow from his boots on the driveway, a pointless endeavor considering the snow was piling up there too.

"Back window is broken," he said, matter of fact. "Tracks in the yard, but they're partially obscured by the blowing snow. I think whoever it was is now gone." He sniffed. "You said the Greens are out of town?"

"Yes, they asked my family to keep an eye on the house. It's on the market." The last part seemed like an obvious thing to add, considering the huge smiling face of an agent plastered on the sign in the front yard.

"Do you have a key to their house?" he asked.

Dread twisted in her gut at the thought of going back inside her house to retrieve it. She really should have left a light on. "I do."

"Did you want me to come inside with you to get it?" Apparently, Danny was a mind reader.

Hannah laughed, unable to hide her nervousness. "No, no." She waved a hand, far more carefree than she felt. "I'll run in quick and get it." Before she completely lost her nerve, she darted back into her house, fumbling with the key before it finally slid into the lock. She flicked on the kitchen light, chasing all the shadows back into the far corners. Through the back window, she could see kitty corner to Jayne's shadowy backyard.

Maybe someone knew they were all going to be at the dance competition and took the opportunity to break in. But who...?

She snagged the keys from the hook on the kitchen wall next to the portable wall phone—her family was probably one of the last landline holdouts—and ran back out to meet Danny in the Greens' driveway. He unlocked her neighbor's side door and pushed it open. "Wait there."

"Mind if I come with you?" she asked quickly. "It's cold out here." *And I'm kinda freaked out*, but she didn't admit that.

"Good idea," Danny said, tipping his head toward the inside.

What a nice guy. (Like, why, *why* did Jayne keep this guy at arm's length?)

Danny held out his hand and guided her by the small of the back into the small side entrance, before taking the two short steps into the kitchen. "Wait in here while I check things out."

Hannah swallowed around a lump in her throat. The stale smell of old garbage in a closed-up house assaulted her nose. Danny moved down the back hallway, leading to the bedrooms. The houses in this neighborhood had been built in the '60s (according to her elderly neighbor on the other side) and there had been only three designs. Hannah's house and the Greens' were mirror images of each other. Behind the Greens' house sat the Murphys' two-story model. She and Jayne had discussed how this would make it easy for a bad guy to stake out a house with complete knowledge of the layout. *Enough with all the crime shows.*

Danny returned a few minutes later. "House is empty, but the smashed window is in Melinda's old bedroom." He held out a decorative rock in his gloved hand.

"That looks like it came from Jayne's garden." Hannah furrowed her brow. "Why would someone do that?"

Danny sighed. "Who knows. Have you seen anyone suspicious around here lately?"

Hannah thought back. "No, not at all. Only tonight. I was about to get into my car and something caught my eye." She shrugged. "I heard the crash, but all I saw were shadows. It's so dark back there. So I called you."

He seemed to be holding something back. "I'll get the house secured. You're free to go." He paused a second. "If you think of anything else, call me."

Hannah turned to leave, then spun back around. "Um, thanks, Danny."

"Just doing my job."

Hannah departed through the side door and jogged to her car parked in the adjacent driveway. She grabbed the snow brush and was clearing the windshield when the hairs on the back of her neck prickled again. She turned around and stared toward the yard. The inky blackness and the snow whipping into her eyes made it impossible to see, but if someone was back there, the motion-sensing light in the eaves on the side of the house would light Hannah up.

An easy target.

Hannah yanked open the door and jumped into her car, flipping the lock switch. She didn't care if she had to drive through three-foot drifts to make it to the dance competition in Niagara Falls. She was not staying home alone tonight.

CHAPTER FOUR

Standing in the Greens' living room in front of their large picture window, Danny tracked Hannah's vehicle as the tires struggled to gain purchase on the snowy residential street. Fortunately, the main roads tended to be treated with salt first, so hopefully she'd be okay driving to Niagara Falls. He dropped the drape, sending the closed-up house into heavy shadow, save for the overhead light he'd turned on in the kitchen. He considered texting Jayne to let her know her friend was on the way, but he supposed that was exactly the type of thing that had strained their relationship in the first place. Jayne claimed he was overly protective, interfering, and a detriment to her job as a private investigator.

Don't hold anything back, would ya?

The harsh words clung to him. How was he supposed to care for her and not want to protect her? He had already failed when it came to her brother—his best friend and police partner. Patrick had been killed in the line of duty. Danny couldn't allow another Murphy to be hurt, not on his watch.

Yet Jayne insisted that she wasn't his responsibility.

So, here they were, taking another break in their fledgling relationship.

Danny sighed heavily and dug a pair of latex gloves out of his back pocket. Being in this house slammed him back to another moment in time. This past fall, he'd had to notify Mrs. Green of her daughter's death in what had appeared, at the time, to be a tragic car accident. He couldn't imagine the heartache the family must be suffering since the truth came out.

Danny had already notified dispatch that he was investigating the scene and he expected another officer would arrive soon. In the meantime, he headed down the back hallway toward the bedrooms. The first bedroom door yawned open. It appeared to be a den of sorts. Perhaps Mr. Green had used it to watch football games on the big screen TV.

He stepped back into the hallway. The last door on the right was the only other room facing the yard. From the case this past fall, he knew this room had been Melinda's. According to Jayne, Mrs. Green had been keeping it as a shrine of sorts. And that's what had been bugging him since he first came into this room earlier to investigate the broken window. It didn't look like a shrine. It looked like someone had been living here.

A knot tightened in his gut as he twisted the knob. Adrenaline had propelled him forward earlier when he had to make sure the house was empty, but now he had time to feel all his emotions. The grief and sadness in this house were palpable. *Just get the job done.* He pushed open the door and a burst of frigid air rushed into the hallway. The snow had increased in intensity and was blowing into the room through the broken window.

The bed was unmade and the covers were tossed like someone had been sleeping in it recently. He opened and closed the closet doors. He couldn't tell if anything was missing or out of place. A stiff wind rustled the papers on the desk.

Danny glanced around for a piece of cardboard or something to cover the window with until he could get the emergency closure services out here. He'd also have to notify the Greens. The police department had all their contact information in their files after their daughter's death.

He found a laminated folder with the image of some male pop star on Melinda's desk. It might do the trick. He opened the drawer and rummaged around until he found packing tape. Luck was on his side.

The light from the bedroom spilled outside onto the freshly fallen snow. Any hint of footsteps, including his own, had been erased. His mind flashed back to the voyeuristic photos Kyle Duggan, the recently re-elected mayor's son, had taken of his ex-girlfriend from outside this same window. What was that kid up to now? Danny made a mental note to check up on him.

Danny got to work securing the window—well, at least, keeping the weather out. Temporarily anyway. A long strip of packing tape came off the roll with a loud rip that scraped across his nerves in the eerily still bedroom. Across the yard sat the Murphy's house, his second childhood home. Shoving aside his wandering thoughts, he finished the task and made a call to the professionals to secure the scene. He didn't like this one bit. Someone harassing a grieving family was the worst kind of evil.

A knock on the side door had him spinning around. He jogged back to the kitchen, where he found his boss, acting Chief Finn Murphy, Jayne's older brother, letting himself in through the unlocked door.

"Hi, Chief." It was odd to call someone by the title his

own father had held for as long as he could remember until recently. On paper, his father had retired, but his hand had been forced after some serious ethics violations. Despite not having the best relationship with his father, Danny did feel a twinge of empathy for the man. He was, after all, his father, and being a police officer had been his whole world. Some seriously questionable decisions had changed the course of his life.

"What did you find?" Finn asked, all business.

"Someone tossed a rock into the back bedroom window."

Finn ran a hand across his chin. "Seriously? Maybe it's time I got my mother out of this neighborhood." He tipped his head and looked across the yard at his childhood home. "Who reported it?"

"The next-door neighbor, Hannah. Only heard the sound. Didn't see anything."

"You talk to my sister? She'd have a perfect view of the yard."

"Jayne and your mom are at a dance competition in Niagara Falls." There was something a little awkward about telling a man details about his own family. Miss Natalie's sons should have had a more active role in their mother's life now that she was sick. But then again, the Murphy men tended to be sexist, expecting their little sister to take care of that sort of thing.

"On a night like tonight? My mom shouldn't be out in this." Finn drew back his shoulders and shook his head in disgust. Danny was growing to admire Jayne more and more. It took a lot of fortitude to come out as strong as she had with all the overbearing men in her life.

Guilt niggled at him. Danny hadn't exactly been what Jayne needed; instead he had been exactly what she already had with her older brothers.

"What's your take on things?" Finn asked.

"The broken window is in Melinda's old room. I don't think it's a coincidence."

"You're thinking a punk is taking advantage of an empty house? Perhaps knows the history here."

"Maybe, but something else bothers me," Danny added. "Come with me." He led Finn to the bedroom. "The bed looks slept in. And as far as I know, the Greens' kept that room exactly how it was after Melinda died.

"I take it Melinda made her bed?" Finn asked. "Maybe she was a slob. Or maybe the grieving mother sleeps here."

Danny nodded. All possibilities. Hearing his supervisor poke holes in his theory made him uneasy. *A messy bed is your clue?* his father's voice boomed condescendingly in his head.

"I made a few phone calls on the drive over," Finn said. "Turns out Carole Anne Green hired a new lawyer and she got out on bail."

Danny's heart dropped. "When? How?" He clamped his lips together, not wanting to sound as flustered as he probably already did. *Why didn't he know?* He wouldn't have any reasonable expectation to be notified. He was just another patrol officer who happened to make the arrest when Carol Anne was finally apprehended. "I thought her mental health was being evaluated. That she was to remain in custody until trial."

"You're not wrong. But her new lawyer got her out to await trial," Finn said. "Apparently, the Greens were sent a certified letter that remained undelivered. Efforts to contact them fell through the cracks." He lifted a shoulder. "Bureaucracy."

"Do you think this could have been Carol Anne?" Danny glanced around and wondered if any of this had to do with the unstable woman who had killed her stepsister. "I need to do a more thorough check of the house. Make sure no one is here."

Finn nodded his agreement. "I'll take the first floor. You check the basement."

Danny had already searched the main floor, but it couldn't hurt for them to give the house another once over.

CHAPTER FIVE

The elevator doors dinged open on the fourteenth floor. Jayne wasn't thrilled with this particular floor because everyone who took the time to scan the elevator buttons would realize this was actually the thirteenth floor. She wasn't (overly) suspicious, but with the way her life was going, who needed to tempt fate?

Miss Natalie exited the car in a slow shuffle, her shoulders slightly stooped. Jayne's heart sunk. This was going to be a long weekend.

"Our room is down here." Jayne forced a cheery tone and guided her mom gently by her elbow. She waved the plastic key card in front of the control on the door and a green light blinked on. Jayne pushed the door open and quickly realized that the air conditioner was cranked all the way up. She didn't recall leaving it on when they checked in earlier. Jayne rushed across the room and shut it off. The room fell silent, save for the *click-click-click-hiss* of the AC sputtering its last gasp. Crossing her arms over her midsection, she rolled up on her heels, then narrowed her gaze. "Mom, where's your sweater?"

Even as she asked the question, she realized they must

have left it on the chair in the convention center. Her mother had made the sweater years ago and it was one of her favorites. Jayne hated to see it go missing.

Jayne tamped down the frustration bubbling up, realizing how unfair that was. Her mom couldn't help it. Debating how to handle the missing sweater, Jayne checked her phone and was surprised she had never gotten a response from Hannah after Jayne's text. A small part of Jayne hoped she hadn't seen the message and would safely arrive at the hotel to give her a hand.

Jayne pulled back the curtain and her stomach plummeted. The snow had been coming down all this time in thick, wet flakes, the kind that was perfect for making snowmen and forcing cars to careen off the road. Had they been forecasting this much snow? She sent up a silent prayer that Hannah was safe. She didn't want to be responsible if something happened to the young woman. Jayne always felt like she had the world on her shoulders.

Miss Natalie shuffled around the room, looking behind the chair and in the bathroom. Without asking, Jayne knew she was looking for her sweater. Her mother's mind knew she was cold and needed to put something on. The sweater had become her safety blanket of sorts. Could Jayne dare go retrieve it and leave her mother here alone? Her mother was too tired to make the trek down to the lobby and across the tunnel to the convention center. With her mother in tow, it would take *for-ev-er*.

Then as if conjured from her thoughts, she heard a quiet knock on the internal adjoining door. "Hello? Anyone home?"

Jayne scrambled to unlock the door on her side of the adjoining rooms. "Hannah!"

The teen had her backpack slung over her shoulder, and her hair was wet from the snow. Jayne pulled her into a fierce hug. She had never been happier to see someone in her life.

"Ah, you missed me?" Hannah dumped her backpack on her side of the wall in the adjacent hotel room. She raised her eyebrows. "If I never have to drive in the snow again, it'll be too soon."

"I told you not to come. I sent you a text." *Oh, but I'm so glad you did.*

"I wanted to come." Hannah held out her hands as if to say, *And here I am.*

"I'm glad you made it safely." Jayne stepped out of the doorway and gestured to her mother who was sitting in the corner of the room, her tiny frame nearly swallowed up by the blue upholstered chair. "Look who's here!"

Miss Natalie's eyes sparked to life. A tremulous smile slanted her thin lips. "Nice to see you, honey." Her mother tended to use endearments when she couldn't recall someone's name.

Hannah crossed the room and gave the older woman a kiss on the cheek. "We're going to have a great weekend, right?"

Miss Natalie's smile faltered. "Are we on vacation?" It was getting late, adding to her confusion.

"We're at the Superstar Dance Power competition."

"Oh," Miss Natalie said, her forehead furrowing. "Is my friend Dale here?"

Jayne's heart warmed. The mind was an amazing thing. Recalling random bits of information and forgetting others. "Yes, he's announcing the awards. Like always."

"Nice man." Miss Natalie folded one hand over the other and sat primly in the chair.

Jayne turned to Hannah. "Would you mind hanging out here while I run down to the convention center. I think I left Miss Natalie's sweater there.

"Of course." Hannah smiled again, this time the brightness reaching her eyes. "You *did* miss me."

"You're indispensable," Jayne said. "I'll be right back." She turned toward the door.

"Jayne..." Hannah called.

Jayne turned around, her hand on the doorknob.

"You won't be long right?" Hannah said, suddenly hesitant. Strange. So unlike the feisty teen.

"Yes, I'll be right back, I promise." Jayne pulled open the door, but paused again, sensing Hannah was eager to tell her something. "Are you okay? Did something happen?" An unease swept through Jayne.

"Go, we'll talk when you get back. Miss Natalie needs her sweater." They both knew they had to find it or risk her obsessively searching for it.

"Okay." Jayne held up a hand, her fingers splayed. "Five minutes. Maybe ten." Jayne slipped out the door and jogged to the elevator and waited impatiently for it to arrive at the fourteenth floor. She would have taken the stairs if she didn't think it was going to be creepy. And smelly. Deserted cement stairwells always seemed to have a funky smell. Right now, Jayne couldn't tolerate either.

Finally, the doors slid open. She paused a heartbeat when she saw Dale Diamond standing in the corner, drumming his fingers on his pant leg. As always, he was impeccably dressed, his shoes polished. His hair was smooth and neat. The small space smelled of cologne and stale cigarettes, and perhaps a hint of desperation, or maybe Jayne was projecting.

"Hello, Mr. Diamond," Jayne said, "great competition so far."

The man furrowed his brow. She'd guess he was early to mid-sixties, but it was hard to tell. "I agree. Let's hope the weather doesn't put a damper on things. Where are you off to? There aren't any more dances scheduled tonight."

"I have to run back over to the convention center. I think

my mom left her sweater behind." Even as Jayne said it, she realized the man wasn't in the least interested in small talk.

Mr. Diamond turned and seemed to study her closely. "Miss Natalie looks fabulous, but how is she? I've heard rumblings."

Jayne's face flushed. "She's slowing down a bit." She was purposely vague out of respect for her mother's privacy, but obviously word had gotten around. Yet, Jayne suspected Miss Natalie wouldn't be bothered if someone knew she was "getting forgetful." She wouldn't remember. Sadly, that was only a fraction of what this disease was going to do to her sweet mother. Regardless, it bothered Jayne that her mother had been the subject of gossip. But why should that surprise her? Everyone loved to dish.

Mr. Diamond pressed his lips together and nodded. There was a sadness in his eyes, but Jayne realized she had never seen him when he wasn't acting in the capacity of emcee for the competition. She suspected that was a mask he wore on stage. Now, something had made the mask slip. Had it been her? Or perhaps the realization his peers were aging, like he was. Both he and her mother had been at this dance gig for a long, long time.

The awkward silence stretched out a beat too long, making Jayne scramble for something to say. The car stopped on the third floor, but no one got on. "Dancing is her life. She still teaches a few classes a week." Jayne purposely omitted the part about needing an assistant to stay on task while teaching.

"Your mother built a studio that has a fantastic reputation." Mr. Diamond seemed to study her for a moment. "That's a good thing you're doing, helping her. You're running the studio." It was more a statement than a question. The tongues were really wagging.

The elevator doors pinged open and the shiny floor of the

lobby glistened. "I'm not a dancer myself. Haven't danced since I was twelve. I'm somewhat limited in that capacity. I planned to be a police officer, but that didn't happen."

He held out a hand indicating that she exit the elevator first. The key card in his hand had room 1997 on it. Her police training would have told him it wasn't safe to flash his room number. Or maybe that was only for women. "You've made sacrifices for your family," he said while they stepped out into the lobby. "You're a good kid." His tone was reminiscent of the role he played as emcee of the awards ceremonies.

Jayne returned his smile.

He patted his front breast pocket and Jayne wondered if he was headed outside for a smoke. "My daughter's dream in New York City doesn't come cheap. That's why I'm still working away." A whiff of cheap liquor wafted off him.

"Lola is a beautiful dancer." His daughter and her neighbor, Melinda, had connected at competitions and continued their friendship because Buffalo and Tranquility weren't that far away.

He nodded with a faraway look in his eyes, then he glanced down at her. "Maybe someday you can follow that dream, become a police officer."

Jayne stood a little taller. "I am working on getting my PI license." No matter how many times she said it, she wasn't convinced it sounded the same. She had spent her life around cops and they loved talking about police wannabes.

"Really?" The single word was meant to portray surprise, but Jayne suspected he already knew her career path. Something about this entire conversation unnerved her, as if he was trying to get information out of her, but for the life of her she couldn't figure out what that might be.

"Well, have a good night." Jayne flicked her hand in a casual wave, remembering her promise to Hannah that she'd hurry back. She quickened her pace across the lobby. At the far side, a tunnel led to the convention center. Despite being enclosed, the temperature in the tunnel was about twenty degrees cooler than the hotel lobby. She should have grabbed her jacket. When she reached the empty convention center, the hairs on the back of her neck stood up. She glanced around, but all she could see were shadows. She broke into a jog and ran to Room #1, the largest convention center room, and the door slammed behind her, leaving her in a quiet space. Her pulse roared in her ears. She couldn't figure out why she was on edge. Maybe her new life as a PI in training had put her in a state of constant hypervigilance, like the room number thing with Mr. Diamond.

She scanned the rows of empty chairs and let out a breath of relief when she found her mother's cardigan pooled on the concrete floor under where they had been sitting. She picked it up and brushed it off, releasing the smell of her mother's soft floral sent. Unbidden, a sadness washed over her.

What will I do when Mom is unable to dance?

Tears burned the back of her eyes and she brushed away a tear. She turned, and out of the corner of her eye, she thought she saw a watery shape move. Terror zinged through her heart, but by the time her vision cleared, whatever she had seen—or not seen—was gone.

CHAPTER SIX

Nerves jangling, Jayne jogged back through the in-door tunnel that connected the convention center with the hotel and casino. Her exhaustion was making her paranoid and suspicious. That's all it was: a general feeling of disquiet. A constant buzz of anxiety. Outside the smudged windows of the well-traveled tunnel, the snow fell sideways under the streetlights. Another shudder racked through her body. Thank goodness Hannah had made it safely through the weather. And she was glad Hannah was here to keep her and Miss Natalie company.

When Jayne reached the lobby, it was practically empty, save for a few gamblers headed to the casino and a young man standing behind the reservation desk looking bored, glancing down occasionally, probably at the cell phone he had been told not to use during work hours. Bells and electronic voices floated out from gambling machines from the casino entrance on the far side of the lobby. She wondered how many dance teams had arrived before the storm. She dragged a hand through her hair and glanced over her shoulder, still unable to shake the feeling that she was being watched. She slid her arms into her mother's cardigan. She found herself smoothing her hands down the soft sleeves. No wonder her mother loved this sweater. She quickened her pace to the bank of elevators, her head on a swivel.

Jayne had never gambled before and wasn't sure what the appeal was. She certainly didn't have money to blow feeding a machine. And the blinking lights and celebratory sounds seemed like something more appealing to school-age children at a birthday play place rather than the current clientele that seemed to consist of little old ladies with white hair and men who needed walkers and oxygen tanks. Jayne wondered if they realized how hard it was snowing outside—or perhaps they didn't care because they had no intention of leaving their slot machines any time soon.

Jayne was about to turn away when loud celebratory cheers rose above the din of the room. A pretty woman dressed casually in jeans and a Bill's sweatshirt jumped up and down. Her two friends in similar garb were clapping their hands in unison. She must have won big.

Good for you, Buffalo Bills fan.

Jayne was surprised by the casual clothing, mistakenly believing people would dress up at a casino. Not sure why she'd thought that, maybe it was something she had seen on TV. A couple men farther away were dressed in fitted business suits hovering over a man at a table. The dealer waited with an annoyed expression on his face. Perhaps he was ready to deal the cards and didn't appreciate the delay. He had the same look as a cashier waiting for someone to write a check with a pen that didn't work. That's when she realized she recognized the man sitting at the table. *Mr. Diamond.* The well-dressed men stood on either side of him. One seemed to be giving Mr. Diamond news he didn't want to hear—based on his strained expression—and the other one had his hands clasped in front of him, his gaze taking in the room. Something about that man seemed familiar, but she couldn't place him.

Jayne bit her lip, hesitating. She had the odd urge to check on Mr. Diamond, even though a little voice on her shoulder yelled, "Not my circus. Not my monkeys." Something about his body language made her want to rescue him. That was the downside of being empathetic and always trying to do the right thing. Maybe she could say, "Hello." She wrapped the cardigan around her middle and headed toward the casino.

At the entrance, an elderly man in a black security uniform stepped in front of her and held up a shaky hand. "ID, ma'am."

"Oh, I..." She patted her hips, but she knew she didn't have her license on her. She had run out with only the room key. She pointed toward Mr. Diamond, who was shaking his head adamantly at one of the men, his face flushed red. "I only wanted to say hello to a friend. I promise, I'm not gambling."

"No one under twenty-one allowed on the casino floor. ID, please."

Jayne pressed a hand to her neck. "I'm twenty-six. Honestly."

"ID please," he said, unmoved.

"Okay." Jayne took a step backward, still watching Mr. Diamond. Maybe it was just as well. She might have been about to barge in on something important. She was probably reading too much into the situation. "No worries, I'll catch him another time." Jayne spun around and headed to the elevators, but she couldn't shake the feeling that Ron Burgundy was in some sort of jam.

None of her business, she reminded herself. None. This was one of the hazards of training to be a private investigator.

She was far too inquisitive. And this was the trait that was jamming a wedge between her and Danny.

Jayne dragged a hand through her hair. Walking away would make Danny happy. Then again, why did she care? She needed to stop worrying about what other people thought about her.

CHAPTER SEVEN

When Jayne got back to the hotel room, she found Hannah sitting across from her mother at a small table under the window. "Hello," Jayne called, catching her reflection in the mirror on the wall by the door and startled a bit at how much she resembled her mother. Maybe it was the cardigan, or maybe it was the haunted, exhausted look in her blue eyes. Or maybe because they had the same frame. Her mother had spent her life dancing and had the stature of a ballerina. Apparently, Jayne had inherited it because she certainly hadn't worked for it. Everyone had *tut-tutted* her, exclaiming that it was a shame she gave up dancing considering she had a dancer's body. She was a natural. Apparently, it wasn't natural for her to want to follow in her father's footsteps instead.

"I see you found Miss Natalie's sweater," Hannah said, snapping Jayne out of her spiraling thoughts.

"Yep. Right under our chairs." *Thank goodness.* Jayne slid off the cardigan and draped it over her mother's shoulders, immediately missing the soft warmth against her bare arms. Her mother reached up and patted the sweater, as if greeting a long-lost friend. Jayne's gaze drifted to the window. "It's really coming down out there."

"Isn't it great? I love a good snowstorm." Hannah drew her shoulders up to her ears and clapped her hands together silently in a gleeful gesture. "It always makes me think of a snow day when they cancel school." Apparently, the teen had already forgotten her white-knuckle drive from Tranquility to Niagara Falls.

"I'm glad we got hotel rooms for two nights. Hopefully, by then, the weather will have improved and the roads will be clear," Jayne said. She leaned over the table and grabbed the cord of the room-darkening shade and lowered it. Immediately, the room seemed to warm by ten degrees. Out of sight, out of mind.

"I'm sure it will," Hannah said, not seeming too concerned. "Besides, I'd rather be stuck here than at home alone."

Miss Natalie covered a huge yawn and both Jayne and Hannah exchanged knowing glances. "I think it's time for bed," Hannah said.

Without needing to be asked twice, her mother stood and walked toward the bed, then turned around, obviously confused by her unfamiliar surroundings.

"Mom, I'll get your toothbrush and PJs." She opened the top drawer and grabbed her mother's things.

"That would be nice, dear."

"Jayne," Hannah said quietly, "after you're all set here, I need to talk to you." Something flashed in her friend's eyes that made her stomach knot. Hannah had obviously been worried about something when she first arrived, and now Jayne felt guilty for being too distracted by her own concerns.

Jayne stopped unzipping her mother's makeup bag and gave her full attention to Hannah. "Is everything okay?"

"Yeah," Hannah said, unconvincingly. The young woman

stood and tucked her chair under the table. "Come to my room when you're free." She placed her hand on Miss Natalie's arm and brushed a kiss across her cheek. "Night. Get lots of rest because we have big plans tomorrow."

"We do?" Miss Natalie looked at her with wide, vacant eyes. "I think I'd rather stay..." She was probably going to say *home* but couldn't form the word.

"I shouldn't have said anything," Hannah muttered under her breath.

"It's okay." Jayne gestured to the other room with her chin. "I'll be there in a minute."

"I'll put on my jammies."

About fifteen minutes later, Jayne had her mother tucked into bed. Jayne turned off the lights and knocked quietly on the adjoining door before slipping through the narrow opening. Hannah leaned against a pile of pillows on the bed with her ankles crossed, wearing some cute character pajamas that reminded Jayne of the teen's age. Hannah was an old soul.

"Hello, there," Jayne whispered as she strolled into the room.

Hannah tossed her cell phone and it landed with a soft thunk on the bedspread next to her. "Your mom settled in?"

"I think so." Jayne flopped down on the extra bed and stared up at the water-stained popcorn ceiling. Which reminded her that she had broken a cardinal rule: she was laying on top of the bedspread. Like, who knew what was on it. She was too tired to think straight.

She sat up, resigned to take a shower before she climbed under the sheets. "I'm worried this might be one of the last competitions for..." She mouthed the words, "My mom," on the off chance that she'd overhear all the way in the other room. "There's too much going on. She's flustered. I only want her to be involved as long as she's enjoying it."

"It'll be easier now that I'm here. You can focus on the

dancers and I'll hang with Miss Natalie." Hannah hugged her knees to her chest and rocked back into the plush pillows.

"You saw my text before you left, didn't you?" Jayne eyed her suspiciously.

Hannah rubbed her jaw in mock confusion. "What text?"

Jayne held out her hand, indicating the cell phone on the bed, lighting up every few seconds with silent notifications. "That thing is an appendage. There's no way you didn't see my text telling you to stay in Tranquility."

"I don't text and drive." That simple statement, meant to be lighthearted, sucked the air out of the room. Melinda Green had checked her phone moments before she was run off the road. If she hadn't been distracted, would she have been able to control the vehicle? "I mean..." Hannah said, lowering her head, realizing her faux pas.

"I know," Jayne said gently, putting her at ease. "And I appreciate that you came. Were the roads bad?"

"Yes." Hannah laughed nervously. "Horrible. If they're not clear by Sunday, I'm going to catch a ride with you guys."

Jayne laughed.

"I'm serious." Hannah rolled her hands at her wrists. "I had the steering wheel in a death grip. I probably got carpel tunnel."

"I'd be happy to take you home if you don't want to drive. We can figure out what to do about your car. But that's a later problem." Jayne shifted to the edge of the bed to face Hannah. "Tell me. What's going on?"

"The reason I left late is because something happened at the Greens' house." Hannah straightened her legs and fluttered her toes. The tips of her toenails had chips of black paint on them, probably left over from her Goth days.

Jayne tucked her chin. "Melinda's house? It's empty. What happened?" A pool of icy dread gathered in her stomach and she suddenly felt nauseous. *Just when she thought things were going to calm down.*

Hannah held up her palms and shrugged. "The house *is* empty. Someone smashed a back window, though."

A back window. "Whose window?" She didn't have to ask to know the answer. The gaudy floral pattern on the bedspread started to swirl.

"Melinda's old bedroom."

Jayne swallowed. Her mouth was dry. "Did you see who it was?" Her mind raced with the possibilities. The one person who had hated the Greens enough to kill their daughter was locked up.

Hannah shook her head, her strawberry-blonde hair softly falling around her neck and shoulders. If Jayne hadn't seen the transformation from jet-black hair and heavy eyeliner to this fresh-faced young woman, she wouldn't have believed it. "No, I didn't see anyone." Her eyes flared wide. "I was pretty freaked out. My parents weren't home. You and Miss Natalie were here."

"Did you go in their house?" Both Hannah and Jayne had a spare key.

Hannah smiled, but it didn't reach her eyes. "Turns out I'm chicken poop."

"Chicken poop?" Jayne frowned.

"I'm trying not to swear. Turns out I wasn't brave enough to check it out by myself. I called Danny."

"Oh, well, that was smart."

"He was on duty, so it wasn't like he was doing me a favor. I hope that was okay."

Jayne waved her hand. She hated that Hannah felt like she had to walk on eggshells around her when it came to Danny. "Of course it's okay. It was good that you didn't investigate on your own. I'm surprised you didn't call 911."

Hannah shrugged one shoulder.

"What did he discover?" Jayne's fingers itched to check her cell phone, but it was in the other room. Wouldn't Danny have called her, texted her to let her know that something had happened in her own backyard? A whisper of regret crowded in on her. Pushing Danny away to assert her independence could backfire. Creating distance went both ways. Like tonight. Before she had picked a fight with him, he would have called her. Let her know what was going on. And from a more practical standpoint, as a fledgling PI, she'd need someone on the inside at the police department. Was that selfish? Or the truth?

"Not much. Danny checked out the property. I got the key and let him in. I took off to come here while he was securing the window."

"Did someone call the Greens? Let them know?" Jayne hated that this was one more thing on poor Mrs. Green's plate. The woman had been devastated by her daughter's death. She didn't need this.

"I...um..." Hannah stammered, as if embarrassed. "Danny said he'd contact them."

"Of course," Jayne said, not wanting to make Hannah feel more uncomfortable than she was already feeling. Jayne moved to sit next to Hannah, putting her hand on her knee. "I'm glad you're here."

"Me too. I wouldn't have been able to sleep alone in my house tonight."

"It was probably some punks who know the house is empty. Maybe kids out drinking. I'm sure the police will find them. Tranquility prides itself on being one of the safest towns in America."

Hannah scooted back and fluffed the bed pillows. She leaned back and closed her eyes. "I do feel better living near you."

"The feeling is mutual." Jayne took a deep breath, then

checked the time on her smartwatch. "I'll let you get some sleep. Workshops start early tomorrow. I'll get up and supervise the younger teams, and you can come down with Miss Natalie a little later. There's no need to rush her." Jayne stood, then turned around. "Hannah, I can't thank you enough. My mom and I appreciate everything you do for us." A fondness blossomed in her chest. "I couldn't do this without you." Jayne had said it more than once, but as far as she was concerned, she couldn't say it enough.

"I'm sure you'd find a way." Hannah stood and peeled back the covers and climbed under the sheet. "For starters, hit the lights on your way out." She rolled onto her side and plumped the pillow under her head.

"Night." Jayne returned to her room and was relieved at the sound of her mother's steady breathing. She was asleep. Jayne grabbed the tote bag with tomorrow's schedule and her cell phone and went into the bathroom, flipping on the light.

The first thing she did was check her phone. There was a message from her brother, Sean, asking if Mom was going to be around tomorrow so he could stop by with Ava. "I told you we had a competition this weekend already," she whispered into the empty room. Her brothers never seemed to remember the details. No, that was her job. She was the one that had to juggle all the balls. Her growing agitation was evident in the dull headache pounding behind her eyes. If she wasn't careful, she'd get a migraine. She did *not* need that.

Jayne clicked through the rest of her texts. Mostly questions from moms too lazy to read the detailed e-mails she had sent prior to the competition. Shooting off a text was so much easier.

No messages from Danny.

Disappointment settled in her gut. *You wanted to be left alone, right?*

Shaking away her disappointment, she slid out the dance

schedule and double-checked the times. She got ready for bed, then set her phone alarm. As she was climbing into bed, her phone buzzed. Hope leapt in her heart, but it was quickly dashed. An unfamiliar number.

TEXT (UNKNOWN NUMBER): *Need to talk to you. Meet me at the casino? 11 pm? — Dale Diamond*

Mr. Diamond? What in the world? Had he seen her trying to get into the casino to check on him?

It was almost eleven. Her thumbs hovered over the screen, debating. Mr. Diamond had a reputation in the past for being a bit smarmy and flirtatious with the adult teachers (never the young dancers), but he had been nothing but appropriately friendly to both her and her mother. If Jayne thought he was going to hit on her, she should ignore this message and pretend like she never got it. On the other hand, if there was something going on—she recalled the concern on his face when he was surrounded by the two men in the casino—maybe he needed something. She *had* told him she was a PI in training. Actually, he had made a point to ask her about her new job. Or maybe she was flattering herself that he'd think to call on her in that capacity. How had he found her phone number?

Curiosity had her throwing back the covers. She dipped into the bathroom and jumped into her jeans and ran a brush through her hair. She had made a decision. She wouldn't respond to his text, but she'd head down to the casino and see what he wanted. If the situation looked sketch, she could turn around and come back to bed and go back to plan A, pretending she never saw his message.

Jayne poked her head into the adjoining room. "Hannah," she whispered.

"Uh-huh?" the teen said sleepily.

"I got an odd text from someone from the dance competition. Are you okay here with Miss Natalie while I run down?"

Hannah pushed up on one elbow, the light from Jayne's room cutting across the teen's scrunched-up face. "No problem. Be sure to open the door all the way so I can hear if your mom gets out of bed."

"Thank you."

Jayne ducked back into her room and stuffed her feet into shoes. She paused for a heartbeat at the door and glanced at her mother. A hint of apprehension tightened in her gut. What if her mom slipped out unnoticed?

No, she was safe. She'd be fine. Besides, Jayne wouldn't be long.

CHAPTER EIGHT

Jayne had remembered to snag her wallet before going down and good thing, too, because the tall, thin, elderly security guard was right where she had left him at the entrance to the casino.

She dug out her driver's license. He ran it through some machine, then handed it back to her. "Good luck," he said, in the same disinterested manner with which he had shooed her away earlier.

Jayne thanked him, then made her way into the casino, where the bright patterns on the carpet competed with the flashing lights and explosive visuals on the electronic gambling screens. Yet, the eye was drawn to a solid red path that cut through the middle of the room. Jayne scanned the sea of gray-haired people and wondered why they weren't home watching TV like her mother did most nights. Well, they may as well enjoy their health and mobility while they had it. She wished her mother could enjoy a night out independently. The bells of a machine paying out snapped her out of her maudlin thoughts.

She looked up and easily found the "Registration" sign

hanging over a counter where three bored tellers waited behind a shield of glass with holes for both communication and sliding ID and cash under. Mr. Diamond had texted her while she was coming down in the elevator that he would be waiting at a machine along the back wall, adjacent to registration. Apparently, he had faith that she'd meet him even when she hadn't been so sure herself. He was easy to spot with his thick, dark hair. His index finger repeatedly tapped the large button on the console. That same button on an identical machine read, "Repeat the Bet." The lines zigzagged cross the screen, calculating any possible winnings before he hit it again, as if on autopilot.

Jayne brushed her hand along the green vinyl of an unoccupied stool. She glanced around, wondering if there was some sort of protocol against sitting at a machine that she had no intention of feeding her hard-earned money to.

"Sit down, no one's using it," Mr. Diamond said, apparently sensing her presence. He hit the button again. Once the lines and numbers stopped on the digital machine, he cursed under his breath.

"Not your lucky day?" Jayne asked, studying the screen filled with wolves, fairies, and arrows that meant nothing to her.

"Not my lucky year." He pivoted on his stool, but not before shooting a forlorn look at the screen.

Jayne let out a long breath, feeling uncomfortable by the look of desperation in his eyes. "You wanted to talk?" Her face burned hot and she plucked at her sweatshirt. She wished she hadn't been so curious because then she'd be in bed sleeping instead of squirming under his intense gaze. He seemed to be trying to figure something out.

"Yeah..." Mr. Diamond ran his hands down the thighs of his dress pants. Jayne had never seen him in anything put suits and ties. "You're a private investigator." He leaned close so as not to be overheard, which was unlikely considering the competing, strident noises coming from all the machines around them. Even the ones that stood unused chirped sounds to entice a passerby—*Come feed me money. Win. Win. Win.*

"I'm in training. I don't have my license yet." She hedged her bets, ready to bolt if whatever he wanted from her made her stomach queasy. But why would he? He was a smooth talker but his reputation was solid. As far as Jayne knew, he was still devoted to his dead wife. Besides, Jayne was young enough to be his daughter, or his granddaughter, if he had gotten an early start on parenthood.

"Then you work for a PI?" The hopeful look in his eyes tugged at her heart. Again, her empathy would be her downfall. Despite his over-the-top, bordering-on-cringy showmanship as the emcee at competitions, Mr. Diamond had always, *always* been kind to her mother.

Jayne clasped her hands, tucked them between her thighs, and give him her full attention. "How can I help you?"

Mr. Diamond sighed heavily, but not before looking at his machine again. "Who knew playing these sorts of games could be so…" He shrugged.

Jane almost said, "Addicting," answering for him, but decided against it. She didn't want to come off as judgmental. Did his concern have something to do with gambling? Her brain logged all the possibilities. Was he in debt? Was that what the two men earlier were hassling him about? What would a man who traveled from town to town with dance competitions need with a PI?

"Is there some client confidentiality between us?" Mr. Diamond gestured with his hand back and forth between them. "Do I need to give you money so that we have client privilege?"

Mr. Diamond apparently watched a lot of TV like she

had. "Not necessary. I don't make a habit of discussing my cases." It was Jayne's turn to glance around. "Did you want to talk here?"

"I do." He picked up a cocktail sitting on a small table between the machines that she hadn't noticed before. "I don't have time to waste." Mr. Diamond dragged a hand across his haggard face. The bags under his eyes were more pronounced without his stage makeup and the right lighting. Jayne felt like she was getting a window into a part of his life he had kept well hidden.

Jayne was itching to pepper him with a million questions, but he seemed skittish and was just as likely to tell her to "never mind" as spill his beans, so she kept her mouth shut.

"Superstar Dance Power is thinking about replacing me with..." his upper lip lifted into a snarl, as if he'd gotten a bad taste in his mouth, "...with that small, peppy blonde."

Jayne fought the urge to bristle at his demeaning remark, and she bit back the first comment that popped into her head. She tucked a strand of hair behind her ear. "The young woman that handed the mic to you today?"

"Yeah..." He shook his head in disbelief. Booze wafted from him. "I gave my life, my career to this gig. Do you know what I've given up to be the public face of this competition?"

Jayne was careful to keep her expression inscrutable. She couldn't imagine this had been an easy life, traveling from town to town, being away from his family, but the drunk man in front of her always seemed to be enjoying himself.

"I can't lose my job," Mr. Diamond continued. He reached over and clicked "Repeat the Bet." The screen lit up and all sorts of bells and whistles went off. The numbers climbed on the bottom of the screen.

Jayne angled her head, trying to make sense of what she was looking at. "Big win?"

"Hardly. They figured out if they unleashed all sorts of

noises, people would think winning less than they bet was still a win. Idiots."

Yet here he sat.

Jayne shrugged. She'd never see the attraction. She cleared her throat, suddenly feeling tired, the adrenaline from earlier wearing off. "How can I help you, Mr. Diamond?"

He turned to her, assessing her. "You can call me Dale. You're making me feel old." He raised a bushy eyebrow and seemed to come to some conclusion. He studied the carpet for a beat before meeting her gaze, sadness evident in his bloodshot eyes. "I guess I am old."

Jayne smiled tightly. "You needed something investigated?

"I need you to do some digging on the woman they plan on replacing me with."

"Digging?" What did he expect her to find? "Where does she live? Isn't she in town for the competition? What could I possibly find in that amount of time?" Besides, she had her hands full with her mother's dancers this weekend. She was rationalizing all the reasons she couldn't—didn't want to —help him.

Dale threw back the rest of his drink and flagged down a nearby cocktail waitress. "Amber Mack grew up in Buffalo. The flash of excitement in his eyes unnerved Jayne. "A local PI would be perfect." He rubbed his hands together. "When you told me you were working on getting your license, I felt it was meant to be. I mean, I have a contract with Superstar Dance Power for three more years. But rumor has it, JR wants a younger face." Something dark flashed in his eyes. "I've been the face of SDP for forty years. Doesn't that count for something?" Spittle flew from his lips. "I have a solid reputation."

Jayne narrowed her gaze. "Are you saying this woman doesn't? That she wouldn't be a good representative of the organization?"

He held out his hand and opened his eyes wide in a way drunk people did, over exaggerated and messy. "That's what I need you for," he said, but it sounded like, "ThatswhatI-neeyoufo."

Jayne bit her bottom lip. The PI business had a dark side, but she had hopes of avoiding it. "I'm not sure I'm the person for the job."

Dale Diamond hung his head and rubbed the back of his neck. "I'm good at my job. I don't deserve to lose it. I can't." He patted Jayne on the knee and she found herself pushing away with nowhere to move. "Please think about it. I can give you everything I have so far on Amber."

Jayne slipped off the stool and took a step backward. "Maybe you should hire a lawyer to enforce your contract. That might be the better way to go." Less icky.

He shook his head in disgust. "That could be tied up in court, and meanwhile, I'm out of a job." The cocktail waitress handed him a fresh drink and he stuffed a few bills in the tip glass on her circular drink tray.

"Mr. Diamond...Dale..." Her plea seemed to fall on deaf ears. "Get a good night's sleep. Things will seem better in the morning."

Mr. Diamond reached out and missed her arm by a hair. "What if, what if...Murphy's took home a nice trophy this weekend?" He took a long sip and the ice clinked in the glass. He licked his lips before continuing, "Miss Natalie's reputation will remain intact. It would be good for business." His proposition came out in a drunken rush. She couldn't be sure if this had been his plan—quid pro quo—all along, or if he was flying by the seat of his pants, growing more desperate.

Jayne slowly shook her head, an uneasy feeling blossoming in her belly. "Mr. Diamond, I'd hate to think there's something improper going on with judging..." Her heart raced and she let her words trail off. As far as she knew, the master of ceremonies never had a say in the winners, but what did she know?

Mr. Diamond held up his hands and waved them dismissively. "I'm sorry. Forget what I said. I don't know why I suggested that. I'm just—" He stopped short, but Jayne suspected he was about to use the word *desperate* or *grasping at straws*, but instead, he squared his shoulders and seemed to compose himself. He stuffed a hand into his waistband trying to tuck in a shirttail. "Think about it." Again with the slurred words. *Thinkabutit* "I just need you to investigate Amber. All on the up and up."

CHAPTER NINE

Early Saturday morning, Danny hopped into his truck to check out a hunch. If he hadn't had an all-wheel drive vehicle, he probably wouldn't have been able to navigate the snow-covered gravel road that looped through the Leisure Acres trailer park. He was off duty, but he had to see for himself if Carol Anne had returned to the rundown trailer after she was released. It would be a logical place to find her.

Home.

His truck made fresh tracks through the deep snow. No one had left the trailer park this morning, unless they had gone on foot. They could have left last night before the height of the storm. He scanned the crisp, white snow. No footsteps, no tire tracks. Nothing. Maybe that had been his answer. Anyone who lived here, hadn't come or gone in the past twelve hours.

Or, last night's relentless snowfall had covered all her tracks—in more ways than one.

A snow-covered vehicle was parked in front of the address he had gotten from Chief Murphy. Carol Anne had been unstable and held grudges. Unhealthy grudges. Undoubtedly Jayne was on her list. Still.

Carol Anne had been jealous of her stepsister before running her off the road. After Melinda's death, she'd turned her rage on Jayne, who had been on the receiving end of her father and stepmother's affection. If she was out there doing irrational things—and he had a strong sense that Carol Anne was—he was going to protect Jayne. He wouldn't let the Murphy family down again. When he and the chief had searched the Greens' house last night, other than an unmade bed, they hadn't found anything that suggested they had an unwanted guest. But something felt off. A vibe. A feeling. Maybe Jayne could pinpoint it. Maybe he'd go through the house with her again after this weekend.

Danny shifted into park and climbed out of his truck. He zipped up his jacket to his chin against the arctic air and glanced up. A ridge of dark clouds suggested more snow was on the way. Winters made him wonder why he lived in Western New York. Ah, the summers made up for it.

He took a step toward Carol Anne's trailer, the snow on the ground hitting him mid-calf. On closer inspection, he noticed a slight indentation, as if someone had stepped out onto the small stoop, then gone back inside during the storm. An eerie quiet had settled over the trailer park with the freshly fallen snow. Everything looked crisp and clean. He shuddered. If only it wasn't so darned cold.

The door sounded tinny under his solid knock. Rustling sounded behind the door, then it opened a crack, revealing a partial face.

"Carol Anne?" Danny asked, suddenly wondering what he was going to say to her. It wasn't likely she'd admit to anything. Doing so would put her right back into custody.

She opened the door farther and stuck her head out,

glanced down the snowy lane toward the main road and his pickup truck, then back at him. "I'm not interested."

"Wait!" Danny said, holding up his hand, sensing he was about to get the door slammed in his face.

Her eyes flashed wide and something sinister swum in their depths. "Get off my porch, Officer Nolan." She obviously remembered him from their past interactions. He supposed a person didn't forget the officer who had cuffed and taken them into custody in a rainstorm on the side of the road.

Danny put his boot on the doorframe, preventing her from slamming the door in his face. Apparently resigned, Carol Anne opened the door a little wider and leaned on the frame, putting on an air of disinterest. Her sigh came out in a puff of condensation. She crossed her arms tightly over her chest. She wore a cardigan that looked more like something a woman twice her age would wear. There was a burn hole in the sleeve, as if she had put out a cigarette on her arm. "Listen, I'm trying to put all this nastiness behind me. I want to live a quiet life." Carol Anne was going for the sympathy angle.

"You still have a trial ahead of you." He studied her face, but she was tough to read.

"They'll see that Melinda's death was an accident. I wasn't in my right mind." Her lower lip trembled and tears filled her eyes. Her skin was an unnatural shade of gray, probably from being locked up. "I feel so awful about Melinda. The jury will see that. Contact my lawyer. I'm not talking to you."

Danny wasn't as confident but arguing about her guilt wasn't the point of his visit. Besides, she might be putting on an act. "Did you go out last night?" he asked.

She tilted her head and studied him curiously, her tears suddenly dried. "Yeah, I grabbed some groceries like the rest of Tranquility. You know, stock up on bread and milk before a big storm. Now I guess because you woke me up early, I can have me some French toast." Her smug expression set him on edge. He didn't have to know her sordid history to understand something was off with this young woman. There was something lacking behind those suspicious eyes.

"Did you go anywhere else besides the grocery store?"

She looked at him for a beat, then shook her head. "No."

"You weren't out at your father's house last night?" He decided to ask the question directly. She either hadn't been there, or she was very practiced in lying.

Carol Anne levered off the doorframe and rubbed the back of her neck. "Sadly, my father and I don't have a relationship. And..." she pointed behind her with her thumb... "my mom passed away last month. Only reason I'm out. We lived in this dump, but she had life insurance." The first genuine look swept across her face, but he couldn't quite pinpoint it. Regret? Sadness? Gratitude? "Hired a better lawyer, Thomas H. Park." She lifted her chin suggesting this was a matter of pride. "He's a lot smarter than the public defender I had before. No one cared if I was stuck in the loony bin."

Danny tilted his head. He imagined Carol Anne had heard that expression from someone much older. Maybe someone had seen her losing her grip on things. Maybe they had threatened her with being institutionalized. He sighed. "I'm sorry about your mother."

Carol Anne shrugged, as if she were ambivalent about her mother's death. Maybe she'd been the one who taunted her daughter. Or maybe there was no one to blame for the young woman going off the rails except her own distorted views.

"I imagine one of the conditions of your release is that you have to stay away from your father and stepmother's house." He squared his shoulders and towered over the woman, even from his position a few inches lower on the stoop.

"Like I said, I haven't been by the house." She took a step backward, deeper into the trailer with her hand on the door, ready to slam it. Any pretense of remorse disappeared and her eyes flashed with anger.

"If you get any ideas, know that I'll be watching." Danny raised an eyebrow.

A slow smile spread across her face revealing crooked teeth. "You'll be watching, huh?" She seemed to be enjoying this as if it was a game to her.

"I'm close with the Murphy family," he said.

"Jayne seems to be close to everyone," she said, showing almost no emotion.

Danny removed his foot from the doorway. He wasn't going to get anything from Carol Anne other than the strong sense that the threat of returning to jail hadn't softened her. He tipped his head. "Have a nice day, ma'am."

She smirked. "You too."

Danny slowed and turned around, an icy blast of cold air assaulting the exposed flesh of his neck. A shudder raced up his spine. He climbed behind the wheel of his truck and turned on the windshield wipers, watching the freshly fallen snow slide off. A sun-faded curtain rustled on the window of Carol Anne's trailer.

Danny had gotten the woman's attention. Now he needed to make sure she knew he wasn't bluffing when he told her he'd be watching her. If Carol Anne had been bold enough to risk her freedom by breaking the terms of her release, she obviously had nothing to lose.

CHAPTER TEN

The first full day of the Superstar Dance Power competition started on time despite the storm churning outside. Based on the dancers dragging in their rolling suitcases full of costumes to the dressing rooms, a lot of teams must have arrived prior to the storm and were staying at the conference hotel.

Jayne drummed her fingers on the side of the aluminum chair, taking quiet satisfaction in the solid *thump, thump, thump* vibrating through her seat. A popular hip-hop song made it impossible to talk in a conversational tone, so she and Miss Natalie sat in silence save for the occasional brief exchange.

"Are we at a party?" her mother asked. *We're at a dance competition, but it feels like a party, right?*

"Are you dancing, dear?" *Not today, Mom. Or any other day.*

"Should we be lining up the girls for their dance?" This had been the most lucid question her mother had asked, to which Jayne let her know that Miss Quinn, one of the dance teachers, had it covered.

Jayne checked her watch. The awards hadn't been scheduled to start for another thirty minutes, but the schedule was merely a suggestion. Sometimes the event ran early, sometimes late. Some of the listed numbers had been skipped. Jayne suspected these teams didn't make it due to the snowstorm. But Dale Diamond knew the variability in the schedule better than anyone, which made his absence even more puzzling. Their conversation last night had made for a restless sleep. Even though she hadn't accepted his offer to fix the competition, she feared that even a whiff of impropriety would tarnish her mother's studio.

He'd been drunk and didn't mean it. Anyone could see that. He was simply feeling sorry for himself. An older man seeing the end of his career, save for the remainder of his three-year contract. A contract they'd likely break.

Jayne took in the sea of eager dance parents awaiting the results for the small groups who had competed first thing this morning. The awards ceremony couldn't start until Mr. Diamond arrived.

On stage, the dancers were having a good time improvising to a Top-40 song. Angling her head, she could see a young woman—Mr. Diamond's purported replacement—smoothing a hand across her stylishly cut blonde hair. She lifted her cell phone, probably on selfie mode to check her teeth.

Impatience had Jayne leaning over to yell above the music. "I wonder where Mr. Diamond is."

Miss Natalie's eyes flared wide, then she scrunched up her face in confusion. She scooted to the edge of her metal chair and looked around. "I think I'm supposed to line up the team." The statement was appropriate for the venue, but the vacancy in her mother's eyes indicated she didn't know any more than that. Jayne was immediately sorry she had brought up her concerns. Old habits die hard. Jayne would forever miss having her mom—the mom she grew up with—to confide in.

Jayne placed her hand on her mother's knee and gently squeezed. "Everything's running smoothly. Our dancers are up on stage waiting for the awards ceremony." Cindy and Paige sat huddled in the back with some of the older girls, apparently too cool to break out and act silly like most of the other dancers.

Jayne's mother sighed her frustration and lifted a shaky hand to cover her ears. "The music is much too loud. You'd think Dale would hurry up and get to it. The man likes to make a grand entrance."

Jayne smiled, happy her mother remembered her longtime friend's name. Jayne shifted again, hoping to see the debonaire emcee racing across the convention center to the stage, making apologies for his tardiness. Instead, her gaze found Hannah. Since Miss Natalie had been up and ready by the time Jayne wanted to leave, Jayne had told Hannah to sleep in and meet them whenever she got up.

"What's the hold up?" Hannah asked, her freshly washed hair pulled into a pony. She had on a cute pink, long-sleeved T-shirt and fitted jeans.

Jayne tapped the glossy brochure showcasing the weekend's events against her thigh. "They're waiting for Mr. Diamond."

Hannah shrugged, then pointed toward the stage with her thumb. "Looks like Barbie is going to take over."

Jayne rolled her eyes, not wanting to encourage her. They both turned and watched the woman strut out onto the stage, confident in a fitted shirt, expensive leggings, and tall red stilettos that Jayne would have broken her ankle in. If the woman wasn't a former dancer, she certainly played the part. She grasped the edges of the stand with both hands, her long, red, manicured nails matching her shoes. She looked left, then right, then leaned toward the mic. "Good morning, Niagara Falls. My name is Amber Mack. Are you ready to get his started?"

The crowd joined the dancers on the stage in a loud cheer. Apparently, Jayne wasn't the only one eager to get this show on the road, but where was Mr. Diamond? Had the convention decided to get rid of him already? It didn't seem likely. Why do it mid-convention? And Mr. Diamond had a contract.

"Hannah, can you stay here with Miss Natalie? I'm going to track down Mr. Diamond."

"Why?" Hannah held out her palm. "Seems they have someone else." Then, without waiting for an answer, she shrugged. "Go, we're fine."

"Take note of where our dancers place, okay? Their moms are bound to ask me why they placed where they placed." Jayne handed off the schedule and a pen. "The announcer will go through them in order. Then write, gold, high gold, platinum, whatever next to the dance. Easy peasy."

Hannah took the brochure with trepidation, then laughed. "How hard could it be?"

With that settled, Jayne made her way through the convention center, keeping her eyes open for Mr. Diamond. Generally, he was easy to spot, his six-foot-five frame rising above most dancers and their families. She slowed at the photography booth set up with a series of monitors for parents and dancers to view snapshots of the performances.

Another moneymaker, Jayne thought ruefully.

Grasping at straws, she approached one of the workers. "Have you seen Mr. Diamond this morning?" She tried to sound breezy but feared she had fallen short.

The older woman was dressed in a blue golf shirt with the SDP logo on the breast pocket. The employees tended to travel from town to town with the organization. The woman held up her finger, indicating Jayne needed to hold on a minute. The woman wrote something down, then stood. "Isn't he in there?" She paused, clearly listening to the cheering sounds. "Is that Amber?" The woman's mouth formed a perfect, "O." The woman's face twisted in obvious disgust. "Why is she on?"

"You know Amber Mack?"

"I only know of her." The woman waved her hand. "Rumors." She shrugged. "I never believed half of it, but sitting behind the monitors all day, I hear all sorts of things. They forget I'm here while they're scrolling through the photos."

"Parents talk about this sort of thing?" Jayne asked, trying to fit some of the pieces together. She knew the moms were especially gossipy, but how did they know the inner workings of the employees of SDP?

"They're not the only ones who check out photos. Studio owners, judges, lots of people...and they talk. And since I'm bored, I listen."

"What do they say?" Jayne didn't expect the woman to do anything other than speculate, but mostly she was wondering out loud. None of this sat right, especially after Jayne's conversation with Mr. Diamond last night. He was obviously distraught over the possibility of losing this job.

"Amber Mack was jockeying to take over Dale Diamond's job, insisting they needed a fresh face." The woman shrugged. "Dale is a nice man. I'd hate to see him go." She glanced down at her nails. That's when Jayne realized they were chipped. Who was she to talk? She always wore her nails short and unpolished. No fuss, no muss. "Dale's daughter has been in New York City for a few years now. Everyone thought he'd retire and move there permanently. But she's still struggling to breakthrough."

"It's tough to make it in dance." In any creative field.

"I heard Dale was supporting her. If he loses this job, his daughter will probably have to give up her dream of dancing on Broadway." Jayne had heard a similar take directly from Mr. Diamond.

The niggling sense of unease was like a bur in Jayne's side. Her face flushed. She tried to avoid gossipy situations, yet she had plopped herself down in the middle of the juiciest gossip. But for some reason, this didn't seem harmless.

"I hope everything works out for him." Jayne raised her hand in a casual wave. "I'm going to see if I can find him. See why he's not on stage." She walked briskly through the connecting tunnel and into the hotel.

"1997. 1997. 1997." She repeated the room number from Dale Diamond's keycard folder under her breath. It seemed to take an eternity to get to the nineteenth floor. If the man was distraught over losing his job, she wanted to make sure he was okay. The elevator door dinged open and she paused, a wave of foreboding washing over her.

Maybe I should call the police. Maybe...

The squeaking wheels of a housekeeping cart sounded from somewhere on the quiet hall. She followed the wall placards for rooms 1951-99. When she turned the corner, a young man in a crisp, clean uniform smiled at her as he grabbed a stack of fresh towels before ducking into a room.

Jayne found herself smiling back, even as her nerves buzzed with adrenaline, fearful of what she might find. 1997 was two doors down. She swallowed, her pulse thundering in her ears. What if she had totally misread the situation? What if Mr. Diamond had been fired early this morning, and now, she was here to add insult to injury by making him tell her he'd been fired? Or maybe the young woman and Mr. Diamond were going to share master of ceremony duties and he was enjoying a leisurely morning. Maybe she had overreacted.

Maybe you should mind your own business.

You wouldn't make a very good PI, then, would you? She argued with herself. Worst case, she'd knock on his hotel door, find a dejected Mr. Diamond watching morning TV and contemplating his future, she'd apologize for bothering him, and she'd be on her way.

Yeah, it wasn't going to go that way. She could feel it in every inch of her being. She always had this kind of sixth sense when something bad was about to happen, like when she was fifteen and her dad had died. And the morning her brother had been killed in the line of duty, she had woken up with a wicked stomachache. Over the years, she tried to ignore her intuition, but it was rarely wrong. That's why she almost spun around and went back down to the front desk. They could send someone up to check on him.

Come on, Jayne. You're already here.

Before she lost her nerve, she lifted her hand and knocked confidently on the door to Room 1997. No sound. No rustling. Nothing.

Oh, man.

"Mr. Diamond, it's Jayne Murphy." When he answered the door, she could pretend she had come up to ask about his job offer last night. Then what? She wouldn't take it. Digging up dirt to destroy a person was way below her threshold for accepting a job. Teddy might bite— "Who refuses a paying customer?" he'd say—but Jayne wouldn't be able to live with herself.

You dug up dirt on Mr. Wentworth. He was cheating on his wife, though.

The squeaking wheels drew her attention away from the door. The young man slowed when he saw her, apparently ready to clean Mr. Diamond's room. "I can come back later."

"Um, no," Jayne said, "go ahead. I'm not..." Her cell phone vibrated in her back pocket, distracting her for a heartbeat, but it'd wait. She had to get into the room. Check on Mr. Diamond. "Um..." she pointed at the closed door, "I was looking for the man that's staying here."

The young man looked at her blankly. "Did you try knocking?"

Heat flared in her cheeks, and she bit back a snappy retort. She cleared her throat and continued, ignoring the absurdity of his comment. *Of course she knocked.* "He didn't answer." She drew in a deep breath. "He was due at the convention center."

The kid's eyes lit up appreciatively. "You with all those dancers? Lots of girls in frilly costumes running around."

Jayne lifted her gaze, landing on his name tag—*Garrett*—then locked eyes with him. She imagined shooting him daggers with an unmistakable message: don't be looking at little girls, buddy. However, she suspected she didn't appear that threatening to a person who might have the propensity to engage in such activities. Mr. Wysocki had told her she had to work on being tough. People didn't give up information to someone who didn't seem too eager to get it. She also figured Garrett wouldn't help her if she made any comments about why he'd noticed the dancers. Though to be fair, it was hard to miss them with their Rac n Roll dance bags filled with fifteen costume changes, their bright red lips, and hair plastered back in neat buns. There didn't necessarily need to be something creepy about his observation.

"Yes," Jayne said, never straying from eye contact, "I'm with the dancers. And Mr. Diamond is the announcer. He'd never miss the awards ceremony." Saying the words out loud sent a shiver coursing down her spine.

"I'm about to clean this room." He lifted the master keycard attached to a retractable cord on his belt. (Everyone should have their keys on a retractable cord, Jayne thought. No more digging for them in the bottom of her overflowing purse. But that was neither here nor there right now.) Jayne stepped aside and Garrett knocked briskly on the door and called, "Housekeeping."

Jayne's heart thrummed wildly in her chest as they waited.

When no one answered, Garrett stepped back and paused at his cart. He patted the pile of towels, seemingly debating something internally with himself. "Do you think he might be dead in there?"

Jayne furrowed her brow. "What? No!" She gestured generally in the direction of Mr. Diamond's room. *Isn't that exactly what she was worried about? But why did he jump to that conclusion so quickly.*

"A few months ago, I found an old lady." Emotion flickered across his face, a combination of horror and *I'll never be able to unsee what I saw.* "She was face down on the carpet. I hate to think how long she might have been there." He shuddered, as if reliving the experience.

"I'm sorry." Jayne took a step forward. That explained his fear. "Want me to check the room?"

Garrett's eyes moved from the door, to Jayne, and back. "I'd probably get in trouble for letting you into a guest's room."

Jayne decided to play it cool. "I'll wait here." She backed up and leaned against the wall opposite Mr. Diamond's hotel door. The sturdy wallpaper was rough to the touch.

Garrett waved his housekeeping pass in front of the lock and it clicked. He shot her a wary glance over his shoulder before apparently gathering his nerve and slipping into the room. A few seconds later, he came out. "Not here. Maybe your friend passed you in the elevators." He shrugged. "It happens."

Jayne let out a breath, relieved. "Do you mind if I go in?" She wasn't sure why she felt compelled to check for herself.

Garrett didn't answer. He grabbed a rag and a bottle of

cleaning solution from the cart and Jayne went into the room before he changed his mind. He followed her in and went directly to the bathroom. The beds were made, as if no one had slept in them. Did Mr. Diamond make it back to his room last night?

"Thank—"

"I'm going to be sick!" Garrett rushed out of the bathroom covering his mouth, his eyes wide with horror. "I hate this stupid job."

CHAPTER ELEVEN

"Ambulance," Jayne yelled. "Call an ambulance!"

Garrett ran between the queen beds and snatched the phone from the nightstand. Jayne braced herself on the bathroom doorframe. She could hear snippets of the phone call over the roaring in her head. "Niagara Falls. Hotel. Room 1997... Hurry."

A pool of blood had partially dried under Mr. Diamond's head. A hunk of hair flopped over, revealing the edge of his toupee. *She knew it!* Holding her breath, she stepped into the bathroom, then instinctively backtracked when glass crunched under her foot. She was potentially contaminating a crime scene. But she had to check his vitals. Watching her footing, she pressed a hand to his neck. The expression "cold to the touch" came to mind.

No pulse.

Jayne closed her eyes and prayed, "Please let me be wrong. Come on, Mr. Diamond."

"Is he dead?" the kid said from outside the door. "Oh man, oh man, oh man, he's dead. Isn't he?" The housekeeper's growing panic wasn't doing anything to help Jayne remain calm. Who was she kidding? Calm wasn't in her nature. So, this situation threatened to have Jayne spiraling into a full-blown, trouble breathing, star-seeing panic attack.

"Is there an ambulance on the way?" Jayne stood and struggled to take the scene in objectively.

Same clothes as last night.

A broken drinking glass by his feet. Amber liquid pooled. Dark, dark red blood under his head. He'd been there awhile. A familiar nagging helplessness threatened to consume her. Had she missed something last night? Had he been trying to tell her something more? Or had he asked her exactly what he'd wanted to ask her: to dig up dirt on Amber Mack?

"This job sucks." Garrett shook his head, the distraught expression on his face making him look younger than he had a few minutes ago in the hall. "I wish people wouldn't do this." He had his back to the bathroom. To Mr. Diamond's body.

"Die in hotel rooms?"

"The worst are the ones that off themselves."

"You think the old lady you found killed herself?"

"I don't know about her. She probably died because she was old." He sounded oddly dispassionate. "In the past two months, two other people offed themselves in this hotel. Linda found both. She quit after the second. People seem to think it's a good idea. On the surface, yeah, this way, their family doesn't find them." He pressed the back of his hand to his nose and glanced over his shoulder toward the body without actually looking at it. At Mr. Diamond. "These poor people never consider the person who has to clean up the mess."

Sadly, despair clouded people's thinking. They weren't considering anything other than ending their suffering. But that was a discussion for another day.

Jayne glanced down. Mr. Diamond's scuffed shoes caught

her attention. What was left of the air got sucked out of the room. Her head spun. "You think he hurt himself?" Her choice of words seemed benign for the situation at hand. *Isn't that why she had raced up to his room? She had been worried about him.*

The young man shrugged. "Was he a gambler? Sometimes people get way in over their heads and see no way out." Garrett picked up the folded towels he had set on the bed. Jayne hoped he wouldn't put them in someone else's room. She shook away the thought—that wasn't her problem.

Garrett looked around nervously, as if finally absorbing the gravity of the situation. "You need to go. I have to secure the room and wait for the ambulance and police." They both knew it was too late for the ambulance.

Her pulse like a ticking time bomb beat in her head. "Why don't you go meet the police at the elevator? Direct them to the room. I'll, um...stay with Mr. Diamond."

Garrett looked at her curiously. "I'm sure he wouldn't know the difference." He checked his watch and sighed. "I have so much work to do. I don't want to stay late. I have plans." Jayne suspected this was just nervous chatter not meant to be disrespectful. He shook his head, then stormed out of the room.

Jayne stepped out of the bathroom and carefully inspected the items in plain view. Mr. Diamond's suitcase was unzipped, but the flap was closed over. She lifted the lid with the tip of her index finger, as if it were a snake that might strike, sinking its fangs into her flesh. The scent of Old Spice —that surprisingly took her back to memories of her dad— floated out. Without touching anything else, she took note of his neatly folded clothing in his suitcase. This was a man who had barely checked into his room. Did that mean anything?

The sound of footsteps and a shoulder radio squawking had her spinning around. She took a few quick photos of the room. Just as she snapped the last photo, an officer appeared in the doorway with his hand near his utility belt. Hovering above his gun. "Who are you?"

Instinctively, Jayne turned around with her hands up, one still clutching her cell phone. "Jayne Murphy. I...um...I came to check on Mr. Diamond. Housekeeping found him on the bathroom floor." She omitted the part about Garrett letting her into the room. No need to get him into trouble.

The officer narrowed his gaze. "I'll need you to step into the hall and wait there." He pointed at her adamantly for emphasis. "Don't think about taking off."

Holding her hands in plain view, Jayne breezed past the officer, taking one last view of Mr. Diamond on the floor. *Poor man.* She was missing something that she couldn't put her finger on. The sound of vacuuming floated down the hall. Garrett wasn't kidding about getting back to work. She placed her hands behind her back and leaned against the wall. And waited.

The paramedics and another officer arrived on the scene, seemingly oblivious to her. Her cell phone vibrated and she glanced at the screen. There was a message from Hannah: *Danny is looking for you. He's here.*

Jayne rubbed her hand across her forehead. *Strange.*

Then Jayne realized she'd missed a voicemail. She tapped on the screen, debating getting into this now, or waiting until the local police had finished questioning her. The first officer came out of the room, making the decision for her. "We're going to take you down to the station to answer a few questions."

"I'm here for a dance competition. I...my mother..."

"It shouldn't take long. We have to clear some things up. For starters, why are you taking photos of the scene here."

"I'm a..." Jayne swallowed the words *private investigator*. It never seemed to get her anywhere with law enforcement, and technically, she wasn't here in that capacity. Instead, she sighed and jammed her hand through her hair. Her phone vibrated again. "I didn't do anything wrong."

The officer reached for her forearm. "We can clear it up down at the station."

While the officer led her toward the elevators, she quickly texted Hannah because her text thread was already open.

Lobby. ASAP.

She hoped Hannah could translate her cryptic text.

CHAPTER TWELVE

"What did the text say?" Danny asked Hannah, keeping his voice low out of respect for the dancers onstage.

The young woman glanced down at her phone, as if needing to confirm the text she had just read. "Jayne texted 'Lobby ASAP.'" Hannah held up the screen of her phone. "See?" She kept her voice equally low.

Danny glanced around, unfamiliar with the setup of the convention center. Had something happened? "Where's the hotel?" Dread pulsed through him. He had been able to track down Hannah and Miss Natalie in the main convention center room after Jayne didn't answer her phone. Jayne had been insisting that he needed to trust that she could take care of herself—that had been a major wedge between them of late—but when she hadn't responded to his phone calls, he couldn't help that familiar tightening in his chest. The incident at the Greens' house last night did nothing to quell his concern.

Hannah pointed toward the double doors he'd come through. "Go out there, to your left. The last set of doors leads to a tunnel that connects to the hotel." She nudged him with the same hand that held her phone. "Hurry. I think something's wrong. I'd go myself, but I can't leave Miss Natalie."

Danny nodded. Jayne's mother was watching the dancers on the stage with rapt attention. He had always had a special fondness for the woman, having grown up without a mother. It was a good thing Jayne was doing, taking such good care of her mom. He pulled his gaze away. He didn't have time for ruminating. "I'll text you once I find Jayne. Let her know I'm on my way."

Danny took off in a jog. The air in the tunnel was markedly cooler than the convention center. The snow had started up again, reminding him how much he hated to patrol during the winter. Between driving on the icy roads, answering calls, or pulling drivers over, he couldn't escape the weather. Part of him wondered why he hadn't moved to a warmer climate. He reached the other end of the tunnel and pushed open the door to the lobby, all thoughts of weather and future job opportunities vanishing as he scanned the lobby. A crowd had gathered. Spectators. Something was definitely going on.

He glanced toward the bank of elevators, then the glass-wall entrance. Niagara Falls Police Department patrol cars were lined up along the curb. A group of officers stood in the cold, their noses red and their breaths coming out in clouds of vapor. One was holding Jayne by the forearm with a not too pleased expression.

Danny hustled through the glass door clearly marked with a sign that read, "Use other door." The wind caught it and slammed it back against the wall of windows. No doubt, the reason for the sign.

"Jayne!" Danny called. An officer had his hand on her head

and was about to stuff her into the back of his patrol car while Jayne seemed to be struggling against him.

What in the world?

"Hey, whoa!" Danny held out one hand and dug into his back pocket for his ID. He slowed before he reached them, not wanting to set off any alarm bells.

The officer spun around, still holding Jayne's arm. She didn't appear to be handcuffed. Good sign. The officer held up his hand, mirroring Danny's attempt at a nonthreatening gesture. "Stay right there, sir."

Relief swept over Danny when he recognized the officer from the academy. He immediately complied, familiar with the stress of dealing with an interfering bystander. In this day and age, anything could happen.

"Officer, Sal, I'm sorry, I don't recall your last name," Danny said, holding his hands in clear view, his badge in one hand. "We were in the academy together." He gestured with his badge. "Officer Danny Nolan, Tranquility PD."

The officer paused, keeping his hand solidly on Jayne's arm, but he had stopped trying to force her into the back of his vehicle. He narrowed his gaze, a cross between curiosity and annoyance flashing in his eyes.

"Fiorella," the officer responded, giving Danny the forgotten last name. Officer Fiorella jerked his chin in Danny's direction. "Sure, I remember you." The officer's mouth quirked. "Can we have a reunion later?" The officer dipped his head and winced as the sharp wind assaulted them. Jayne had her arms wrapped around her middle and she implored Danny with her eyes but remained silent. Her entire body was trembling, either from the situation she found herself in, or the cold. Probably both.

"Jayne Murphy is a friend of mine." Danny tilted his head toward the lobby. "Can we go inside and talk? Get out of the cold? Clear this all up?"

"Ms. Murphy was found at the scene of an unattended death taking photographs. I need to take her to the station."

Scene of a death?

The snow intensified and pelted their faces. "Let's go inside. I promise you; Jayne is harmless. This must be a misunderstanding."

"What's going on here?" Another officer approached. "Let's get out of this weather."

"I agree. Let's go inside." Danny reached for Jayne, but the officer wasn't letting go of her.

"We're going to the station." Officer Fiorella insisted.

Danny checked the other officer's name tag. *The chief. Perfect.* "Chief Ross, my name is Danny Nolan. I'm with the Tranquility PD."

Flakes of snow had gathered in his raised bushy eyebrows. "Chief Nolan's son?"

"Yes," Danny said, holding his breath for a beat, wondering if being the former chief's son was going to buy him any points. Before the man had a chance to send him away, Danny said, "Jayne Murphy is a personal friend of mine. I can promise you I'll bring her to the station myself."

The chief tipped his head. "Officer Fiorella, please allow the young woman to go with Officer Nolan. He'll drive her down to the station to answer any questions."

"Chief, she—" the officer said.

The chief held up his hand. "Officer Nolan will make sure Miss Murphy comes down to the station."

"Absolutely." Danny instinctively reached out and took Jayne's arm in almost the same position where the other officer had been holding her. Without waiting for her to respond, he pulled her close and ushered her into the lobby. He was freezing in his winter coat, so Jayne had to be downright numb.

Finally out of the weather, Jayne ducked out from under

his protective arm. "You'll bring me down to the station? How about telling the officer to go pound salt?" Her cheeks fired red and he suspected it wasn't only from the cold.

Danny jerked his head back. "I said what I had to to keep them from stuffing you in the backseat of his cruiser. Tell me, what happened?"

Jayne lowered herself onto the lobby couch and dug her hands into her curly red hair. Her anger seemed to morph into something else. What was going on?

"Dale Diamond is dead," Jayne finally said, her voice cracking.

Danny sat down next to her, eager to pull her chapped hands into his to warm them up, but he resisted the urge. "Who is Dale Diamond? What is this about taking photographs?" He angled his face to try to catch her eye, but she wasn't having it. "Tell me." Had things gotten this bad between them that she wouldn't even confide in him when she was in trouble?

CHAPTER THIRTEEN

Rage muddled Jayne's thoughts. She wasn't quite sure where her anger was directed. At Officer Fiorella who had squeezed her arm so hard she'd probably have black and blue finger marks? Mr. Diamond for getting himself into whatever jam had landed him on the bathroom floor with a pool of blood staining the grout? Or Danny for being able to talk the officer into letting her go when she couldn't?

It wasn't fair to be angry at Danny, but she couldn't help it. Why didn't people listen to her? Why couldn't she command the same authority?

Jayne blinked a few times, then looked over at Danny. He was watching her closely. Gosh, he was handsome. Why couldn't she accept his help? Appreciate him? She sighed heavily, trying to calm her emotions and clear her fuzzy thinking. Because of him, she was sitting in the lobby of the hotel instead of in the back of some stinky patrol car on the way downtown.

Jayne drew in a deep breath. "Thank you for intervening. That jerk wouldn't listen to me. I don't know what he thought I was going to do with the photographs."

"Tell me what happened," Danny said, leaning forward and bracing his arms on his thighs.

Jayne explained how she had found the emcee for the dance competition dead on his hotel bathroom floor. When she finished sharing the details, a new wave of panic washed over her. She scooted to the edge of the couch. "His daughter. Someone needs to contact her before she hears about it on social media." Jayne tuned into the gathering crowd in the lobby and the police cars out front. The ambulance.

The coroner's van.

Surely there would be a lot of speculation among the dancers and their parents. She prayed someone cleared the lobby before they brought Mr. Diamond's body down, otherwise someone would take a photo of the body bag and hashtag it SuperStarDancePower or something that his daughter might find.

Danny's warm hand covered hers, chapped and red from the cold. "Do you have his daughter's number?"

"I can track it down through the organizers." She dreaded making that call. "Hey..." A realization hit her. "Why are you in Niagara Falls anyway?" Her eyes flared wide. A spike of adrenaline made her feel sick. "Did something happen to one of my brothers?" Both were in the Tranquility police department. She knew all too well the tragedy of losing a brother in the line of duty. Her thoughts were spiraling and Danny must have recognized it.

"No, Finn and Sean are fine." He encircled her wrist and gently rubbed his thumb across the inside, sending reassuring vibes—and something more—racing up her arm. "Your family is fine. I promise. Your brothers *and* your mom. I was with Miss Natalie when you sent your SOS to Hannah."

Jayne swallowed. Her throat was parched. "Why are you here?" Of late, their relationship didn't include Danny joining her at a competition just because.

Danny appeared to be debating something internally, and she had an overwhelming urge to rest her cheek on his broad chest and allow him to hold her tight. Forget everything. This morning, she had been reminded once again how quickly life could end. Would insisting on her need to be independent be worth it if something suddenly happened to Danny?

She closed her eyes and drew in a deep breath. She couldn't live her life worried about "what ifs."

"Let's go take care of this mess first," Danny said, "then we'll talk."

Her eyes moved toward the elevators. "Poor Mr. Diamond. I'm beginning to think I need to stop going to dance venues. Last one I was at, a performer plunged to his death onstage." A shudder racked through her. "The Niagara Falls PD isn't going anywhere. We can go down and answer their questions, but right now, you're going to tell me why you happened to be here to rescue me from the overzealous Officer Fiorella in the first place. We can go round and round. You first. Does it have to do with the smashed window at the Greens'? Hannah already told me about it." She tilted her head. "Something tells me a broken window wouldn't bring you here. You could have called me about that."

"And risk it going straight to voicemail?" He arched one brow. Touché.

She shook her head and couldn't help but smile. "I never send your calls to voicemail." *Never* might have been an exaggeration. A flat-out lie.

Danny rolled his eyes and she was happy they had returned to their usual banter, for however long it would last. "Carol Anne is out."

Bam, back to reality!

"She's *what*? I thought her mental health was being evaluated. That she'd be in custody until trial." Jayne's voice grew louder than she had intended. Her stomach ached with all the stress and she wish she hadn't chugged that tall coffee with creamer she'd grabbed from the concession stand inside the convention center. Fearing the inevitable, she scanned the lobby for the nearest ladies' room. She cleared her throat, willing the stomach cramps away. "How could that be?" Knowing the woman who had coldly run her half-sister off the road and killed her—and harbored a certain resentment against Jayne—was locked up until her trial had been a source of relief. The trial had been delayed twice by filings from her court-appointed lawyer, one stating that Carol Anne wasn't of sound mind. "Do you think she's the one who broke the window at her dad's house?"

Danny lifted a hand, his expression noncommittal.

Jayne drew in a deep breath and exhaled. "What aren't you telling me?"

"We need to focus on your problem here first okay? We're going to get your coat, then head to the police station. You have to tell me *exactly* what happened upstairs. Then, if the police ask too many questions, we'll have to consider getting a lawyer."

"A lawyer?" Jayne jerked her chin back. "I didn't do anything." Had she? Was there a law against taking photos?

The memory of Mr. Diamond's body flashed in her mind, defusing her anger and suddenly making her feel very, very sad. "Mr. Diamond is dead," she whispered, afraid of being overheard. With every minute they stood chatting, the greater the risk the news of the older gentleman's demise would reach his loved ones. Having seen details of her brother's death splashed on the local news was painful, even if she had been able to brace for it. She couldn't imagine mindlessly scrolling through Facebook while watching Netflix and stumbling upon the horrible news of the death of a loved one.

"How did you get in his room, anyway?" Danny asked.

"Housekeeping. When I went into the room, I had no

idea he was dead. I walked through his room and the cleaning person found him on the bathroom floor." She stuffed her hands under her armpits and shuddered, the cold finally catching up to her. "I thought I should take some photos in case his death turned out to be sketchy."

"Do you think it was?"

"His shoes were all scuffed up. Like someone dragged his body." Jayne shoved a hand through her hair and her fingers snagged on her curls. That's it! That's what had been bothering her. His shoes.

"Does he have enemies?" Danny asked.

Jayne sighed her frustration. "He told me last night that he was afraid of losing his job." She hated her growing sense of helplessness, like she had missed her one opportunity to change the course of events.

Danny held up his palm. "Tell the police all this. They'll sort it out."

Something about his comment made her bristle. *Let the police sort it out.* Not a wannabe cop like her. She tried to shake her growing feelings of resentment. Now was not the time. A man's life had ended. A kind man who had spent his life chasing a dream that never happened. As a result, he had been determined to make it work for his daughter.

His daughter. "I have to track down his daughter," she said again.

"The police have systems in place for that." Danny tilted his head in a *let's go* gesture. "Let's clear things up with the NFPD." He seemed oblivious to the internal battle she was waging.

"Let me talk to Hannah, then we can leave. Do you think the police station will take long?" She waved him off before he had a chance to answer. It was a silly question. Who knew how long it might take? "I need to let my mom know I'll be back too. She'll be looking for me."

As Jayne and Danny strode through the tunnel to the convention center, a headache began pulsing behind Jayne's eyes. She'd known this weekend was going to be busy, but she had no idea.

No idea at all.

CHAPTER FOURTEEN

By the time Jayne answered the questions at the Niagara Falls police station—questions that could have easily been asked right at the darn hotel—and got back to the said hotel, it was lunchtime. Danny had dropped her off and headed back to Tranquility.

The police were convinced it was an accidental death due to a fall, most likely the result of drinking. Jayne wasn't so sure. But right now, she had to get back to her dancers.

Per the published schedule, the participants were taking an hour lunch before they continued with the large group category. This worked in Jayne's favor because the weather had hampered their travel. Thank goodness Danny had been driving. His four-wheel drive truck handled the deep snow much better than her little sedan would have.

As she rushed to the dancers' dressing room, she rehashed the conversation with the police in her head. They'd wanted to know who found the body and if it had been moved, and they'd somehow known about her conversation with Mr. Diamond last night. They knew he'd been drunk and that she had been with him. Which led her to wonder if someone had been watching her. *But why?* They also asked a lot of questions about how well she knew the man. (Not very.) They seemed to want to convince her that it had been an accidental death. That the poor man had fallen and bashed his head. The police also made her send all the photos from her phone to them, but for some reason, didn't ask her to delete them.

Jayne wasn't a detective, but she understood their line of questioning. Anytime someone died unattended, they had to make sure there wasn't foul play or drug use involved. Hopefully, for the peace of mind of the family, they could rule it a natural death.

Natural.

Nothing was natural about what Jayne witnessed. Yet the police seemed quick to deem it a fall, leading to his death.

"Miss Jayne," one of the younger dancers called to her when she slid through the slit in the curtain that cordoned off a section of the convention center creating a large dressing room. "They canceled the rest of the competition," the girl said. "A lot of the teams couldn't make it because of the weather."

Jayne jerked her head back, startled out of her thoughts. She held out her hand and guided the young dancer toward where the girls had set up their Rac n Rolls, their own personal closets with their vibrant, sparkling costumes neatly hung. Some were eating their packed lunches, others were engrossed in their phones, and some were just talking. Two mothers were having a conversation in whispers while sipping coffee. Jayne could only imagine what—or who—they were talking about. Probably poor Mr. Diamond.

She scanned the faces of the dancers, most everyone seemed present. This year they didn't have any boys on their team, so she could call a meeting in the changing room without leaving anyone out.

Cindy's head snapped up, her mouth had gone slack and all the color had drained from her face. Jayne's eyes were drawn to the phone in the dancer's hand, but the screen was too far away to see what was on it. Jayne could only imagine what had already found its way to the Internet regarding Mr. Diamond.

"Hello, everyone." Jayne smiled tightly, trying to preempt Cindy from saying whatever was on her mind. Jayne wanted to be the one to broach the subject of Mr. Diamond's death. "Does everyone have something to eat?" While some stayed and others left to go about their day to return later, most parents were good about sending their dancers with enough food to snack on during the day.

They nodded their heads and continued to eat.

"I had some errands to run, but I've heard they've canceled the rest of the numbers for today."

"Are we going home?" one dancer asked.

Jayne considered the snowy roads. "We should wait out the storm." Not everyone had a hotel room, but there were enough to accommodate all the girls, if necessary. But she wouldn't suggest that yet. "The crews are pretty good about clearing the snow. We'll wait and see how the roads are in a couple hours." She rubbed the back of her neck. The thought of having a slumber party with the entire dance team was not on the top of her list. *It isn't anywhere on my list.*

"Why did they cancel the competition?" one of the peanut-sized dancers asked. Zoe was going to be a force to be reckoned with if she continued to make dance her priority.

"The weather." The simple statement tasted like the lie that it was.

Zoe looked crestfallen. "My mom went out for lunch. Will she get stuck in the snow?"

Jayne looked toward the dressing room entrance, for no

other reason than knowing that was the way toward outside. "Did some of the other moms go out for lunch?"

A few more dancers nodded, not looking too concerned, so Jayne played it off. "I'm sure they didn't go far. Meanwhile, we're safe and warm here."

The din of conversation rose, the dancers no longer interested in the weather or their missing moms.

Miss Natalie stepped forward, her flowing skirt hugging her thin legs. "Dancers, you need to pay attention. Now, hush."

The dancers immediately quieted down and turned their eyes toward her. Jayne locked gazes with Hannah for a heartbeat and the young woman shrugged. Jayne had to think on her feet. "We'll finish lunch, change into street clothes, and we'll play games."

Some of the older girls groaned. Cindy spoke up. "Can we just use our phones?"

"Um, does everyone have a cell phone?" Dumb question based on the unanimous nodding of heads.

"Would you like to play a group game or hang out on your phones?" She found her shoulders relaxing because she knew what the answer would be. The last thing she wanted to do was play cruise director to a bunch of bored kids.

With that settled, Jayne joined Hannah and her mother. "This weekend didn't turn out how I expected."

Miss Natalie sat down on the edge of a metal folding chair and began leafing through the shiny competition brochure. She glanced up, a frown tugging on her lips. "Shouldn't the team be getting ready for their next number?"

Hannah put her hand on the woman's shoulder. "We'll make sure they're ready."

Once again, Jayne's heart warmed to the young woman whose interactions with Miss Natalie seemed to be second nature.

"Are you hungry, Mom?" Jayne asked.

Miss Natalie's brow furrowed a fraction. Hannah reached into the tote bag resting against a free-standing, full-length mirror. She found an apple cinnamon breakfast bar, opened it, and handed it to her. Miss Natalie ate the bar, then went back to flipping through the schedule.

Hannah took Jayne's arm and dragged her away from where the dancers had set up camp. "Are you okay? What did the police say happened to Mr. Diamond?" Jayne had called Hannah and filled her in when she was waiting at the police station.

"They're convinced his death was an accident. Danny said they ask a lot of questions for an unattended death. That's all." Jayne was willing to be completely forthcoming with Hannah, but not here. Too many ears. She leaned closer. "We'll talk more later."

"I'm glad you're not stuck in jail because I don't think I could manage all these dancers on my own."

Hannah went to high school with some of Miss Natalie's students, and even though they didn't talk about it, Jayne suspected they didn't hang in the same crowd.

Hannah's gaze drifted to the narrow windows at the top of the tall walls. The snow was still coming down. "Since they cancelled the rest of the weekend, do you think we'll get home tonight?"

Jayne drew in a breath and released it. She pulled up the weather forecast on her phone. "Radar doesn't look good. I suppose we should look on the bright side. At least we have a hotel room."

Hannah rolled her eyes. "That we'll be sharing with a half dozen girls. More if their moms don't make it back from lunch."

"Hush!" Jayne said more playfully than she felt. People claimed she was patient—Jayne attributed it to a good game face—but a dance team sleepover might put her over the edge.

"Miss Jayne," Cindy said, zipping up her team jacket and strolling toward them.

"Yeah, hon?"

"Paige said she was meeting a boy. She should have been back by now."

"A boy? Did she leave the building?" A knot twisted in Jayne's belly.

"I don't think so. Paige said she was going to grab a coffee here at the convention center. Want me to look for her?" Cindy's eyes flashed bright, always eager to please in an Eddie Haskell sort of way. Always the TV lover, Jayne had caught a few late-night episodes of the classic, *Leave it to Beaver*.

"No, better you stay here. I'll go," Jayne said. All the girls need to stay together. The way her luck was going, she'd find Paige and lose Cindy. It'd be like a game of Whac-a-Mole. They were her responsibility. Despite her confident tone, a niggling worry made her stomach hurt again. "Cindy, did Paige drive herself to Niagara Falls?" If she had access to a car —in this weather—that could seriously complicate things.

Cindy nodded. "She picked me up. We parked in the parking garage attached to the casino and hotel." Her eyes brightened. "Want me to show you where?" The teen was desperate to go on a mission. "My mom came up in her car later."

"Let's first see if I can locate her inside the building." The headache that was thumping behind Jayne's eyes was turning into a full-blown migraine. *Please let her be in the building.* "Go back with your teammates. Okay?"

Cindy nodded. "Um, Miss Jayne, is it true that someone killed Mr. Diamond?"

Hannah and Jayne exchanged a quick glance. Jayne schooled her expression. "Sadly, Mr. Diamond has passed. No one is in danger; it was an unfortunate accident. And Cindy..."

"Yeah?" the teen replied.

"Try not to mention it in front of the little kids."

"I think they already know," Cindy said, her tone suggesting that not much got past kids nowadays.

"In that case, reassure them that everything will be okay. Can you do that?" Jayne asked.

"Sure, why not." Cindy stuffed her hands into the pockets of her team jacket, spun around and jogged back to her friends."

"Is it?" Hannah asked.

"What?"

"Gonna be okay?"

It was Jayne's turn to shrug. "One can dream."

CHAPTER FIFTEEN

Jayne wanted to crawl into bed and pull the covers over her head. Her eyes felt gritty and heavy. This weekend had been far more than she had bargained for, but as soon as she thought that, she immediately regretted her selfishness. Poor Mr. Diamond hadn't asked for any of this either. And now he was dead.

As Jayne searched the entire convention center, her emotions shifted between apprehension and aggravation. If Paige had taken advantage of all the chaos to see her boyfriend without her parents' knowledge, Jayne was going to —she tempered her response—be very upset. What an understatement. As if her parents already didn't have enough on their plates with their divorce and all.

When Jayne couldn't find Paige in the main convention room, she tried the smaller room where small groups and solos tended to perform. A fresh wave of goosebumps blanketed her skin when she realized sections of lights had been turned off. It seemed most everyone had made their way over to the hotel or to their cars. The empty space felt deserted. She slowed in her tracks and glanced around. Jayne was about to turn around when she heard voices. Urgent. Arguing.

She walked farther into the space and turned to face the stage. Off to the right, Amber Mack was talking to someone who looked familiar, but Jayne couldn't quite place him. She had seen him before. Dressed differently. A completely different vibe.

Where, where, where...

Then it hit her. The man currently dressed in an oversize track suit was the same man who had been impeccably dressed last night talking—arguing?—with Mr. Diamond in the casino. But she knew him from somewhere else, too. The woman stopped talking and turned her focus to Jayne. "Can I help you? The competition has been canceled due to the inclement weather." Her voice was clipped and authoritative, like a schoolteacher, or maybe an evening anchor on the local news. *Maybe this is where fired TV station employees go to ride out their careers.* However, as far as Jayne knew, Mr. Diamond had gone from trying to make it on Broadway as a dancer to a moderately successful spokesperson in the dance competition circuit.

Jayne swallowed hard and approached them. Smiling broadly, she held out her hand. "Hello, I'm Jayne Murphy. My mother owns Murphy's Dance Academy." She wasn't sure why she had said that, but she figured it would give her some credibility and a reason for lingering.

"I'm Amber Mack," the blonde said. Softening a fraction, she held out an open palm to the gentleman standing next to her. "This is JR. He *is* Superstar Dance Power. Perhaps you've met." Amber stopped and smiled, revealing perfect teeth while Jayne shook her head. "He made it in from New York City before this awful weather," Amber continued.

Jayne had never met the man, but now she understood why he seemed so familiar. Where Mr. Diamond was the voice of Superstar Dance Power, JR was the face, owner, and founder. From what Jayne understood, he tended to only hit the bigger cities. The dance competition circuit was so large, that SDP was often in more than one city during any given weekend.

The man tipped his head slightly but didn't accept Jayne's hand. He gave off a very aloof vibe, like he expected her to kiss his ring. Or maybe Jayne was in a foul mood.

Jayne had so many questions on the tip of her tongue, but she decided to ask the only thing that was pressing. "Have you seen a young woman recently? Blonde, willowy, very pretty. I'm trying to find one of my dancers who seems to have wandered off." Jayne glanced around the room even though it was obvious they were alone. For some reason, she sensed Amber and JR had been counting on that.

Amber shook her head. "You've described most of the young women here." She lifted her chin and glanced down at Jayne. She had a very practiced way about her. "But I'm afraid I haven't seen any stragglers."

"Okay, thanks." Jayne went to leave, then turned back around. She wanted to watch their faces when she offered condolences. "I'm sorry about your loss."

The blonde blushed and the older man furrowed his brow as if he didn't understand.

Jayne plowed on, "Dale Diamond was a fixture at Superstar Dance Power. He'll be missed." She added the last bit pointedly.

"Yes, he will be." JR ran a hand over his face, and his gold wedding band caught what little light there was in the space.

Jayne took a step backward and lifted her hand to wave. "Drive safely." She turned to leave when the older man called her name. His tone remained affectless, sending a chill up her spine. She stopped. "Yes?"

"I understand you found him." His dark eyes bore into

hers. Maybe this brooding quality was a personality trait more than a cause for alarm.

"Yes, I did. Tragic." She tried to keep it generic, not to give anything away. "How did you know?"

"I saw you being led out by the police."

Embarrassment heated Jayne's cheeks.

"What were you doing in his hotel room?" JR asked.

"I was worried about him. He didn't show up for the awards ceremony this morning."

"I handled those duties." Amber crossed her arms over her chest and huffed. "It wasn't like his absence was holding anything up."

Jayne angled her head and stared at the woman. When silence stretched a beat too long, Jayne said, "Well, I getter go."

"It seems odd, though," Amber said, "all things considered, doesn't it?"

JR put his hand on Amber's arm in a somewhat possessive way. "It's okay. It's over now."

"You've lost me," Jayne said, trying to keep her voice neutral even as goosebumps raced across her flesh.

Amber dipped her head and spoke quietly, "Surely you've heard. Dale Diamond was being investigated for inappropriate behavior."

Jayne placed a hand on her belly, feeling like she had been sucker punched. Sure, the girls had made jokes about him, called him Ron Burgundy, but the man had always been ethical and professional. Well, he'd been flirtatious with the adult women, never with the children. Had he crossed the line? Was there even a line? No one should be flirtatious on the job.

Period.

As Jayne was trying to process this, Amber lifted her chin. "Mr. Diamond made me feel very uncomfortable."

Jayne swallowed around her dry throat. "Oh, I hadn't heard. That's awful." No one should feel uncomfortable in the workplace. Jayne understood that. There had been some candidates in the police academy who had enjoyed making her squirm with their crude comments. It would probably take a generation or two to retrain some men, if ever.

Had Mr. Diamond been less than truthful with her last night when he was worried about his job? Jayne shook her head, wondering how this day could get any worse.

The man in the tracksuit who apparently ran this entire operation had surprisingly little to say regarding this nightmare unfolding around them. Something niggled at the back of her brain. This might be her one chance to talk to JR before he left town. "Is that what you were confronting Mr. Diamond about last night? Telling him he was fired?" If Mr. Diamond had been guilty of sexual harassment, it would have been a breach of contract. Maybe Mr. Diamond knew all this, but still wanted to get Jayne involved to find something on Amber. A last-ditch effort to save his career.

"Last night?" the man said, pulling off a confused look.

"At the casino."

JR shook his head and sucked his teeth, as if what he was about to say pained him. "I did see Dale last night. He had been drinking. I was trying to get him help. All of this would have made terribly bad press for SDP. And for him."

A loud crash snapped their attention toward the stage. The steel beams clanged as two workers dismantled the stage, more surprising since Jayne thought everyone had left. They must have slipped back in while they were talking.

"We have to be ready for the next city." JR turned to watch the workers.

"Was it unusual for Mr. Diamond to drink?" Jayne asked.

"He'd been sober for years. Shame, really," JR said.

"A real shame," Amber agreed, clutching her hands in

front of her, as if she was trying to refrain from talking with her hands. "We were worried that his alcoholism contributed to his inappropriate behavior."

We. The single word sounded odd coming from the young woman's lips. Were she and the married JR somehow involved? Jayne dismissed the thought. She already had far too much on her plate.

"Well, I hope we have better weather next year," Amber said with a dismissive tone.

An awkward laugh escaped Jayne's lips. "I hope so too." She waved casually and walked away, feeling two sets of eyes on her.

CHAPTER SIXTEEN

A steady surge of anxiety hummed through Jayne's body. Paige was nowhere to be found in the convention center. Jayne held her breath as she entered the dressing room, praying the young woman had magically reappeared. The faces of all the dancers and a couple moms turned to look up at her expectantly.

Hannah rushed up to her. "Any luck?"

Jayne shook her head.

Cindy Peters's mom approached. "Paige's mother always leaves her to her own devices. Like, who allows their teenager to drive all this way in a snowstorm?" The mother shook her head, the air of disdain rolling off her. "I've always picked up the slack." An expensive designer purse hung from the crook of Mrs. Peters's arm as she waved her hands around, emphasizing her point. "Ever since the girls started dance way back in kindergarten."

"I'm sure Tiffany appreciates your help. Her little guy is busy with his activities." Jayne could feel the strain in her smile, and she hoped the judgmental mom would muster up some empathy.

"Well, she's not the only one with more than one child. I have two older sons. I somehow managed."

"You're a real angel," Jayne said, feeling her composure crack. "Do you have any idea where Paige might have gone? I mean, since you've taking responsibility for her. Any ideas at all?" Her tone reeked with the pettiness that was welling up in her soul.

Mrs. Peters clutched the silky fabric at the neckline of her blouse. "The girls are young women. It wasn't my responsibility to watch her. She should have been responsible for herself." The concern in her voice turned hard. This was a woman who insisted on putting her two cents in, as long as she didn't have to do anything.

"If you'll excuse me, Mrs. Peters. I need to talk to the team."

"One more thing," Mrs. Peters said. "Cindy and I checked the parking garage. Paige's car is exactly where they left it."

"Thank you. I appreciate your checking." Some of Jayne's frustration toward the woman disappeared. She cleared her throat and lifted a hand to get the attention of the dancers. "Girls, girls!" The din of chatter died down. Their team was the last one left in the makeshift dressing room. "We have a few things to cover. The weather has gotten worse, and the roads are impassable."

"My mom got us a hotel room because last year there was a lot of snow too," Lily from the mini's team spoke up. She had a fuzzy pink North Face jacket on over her leotard, making her legs covered in black tights look like matchsticks.

"That's great, Lily." If Jayne ever thought she'd missed her calling as a teacher, moments like this reminded her she hadn't. The rest of this weekend was going to test every bit of her patience. "We'll do a headcount in a minute and make sure everyone has a place to sleep tonight." She watched Lily take a bite of a carrot on the side of her mouth, undoubtedly because of the purple brackets on her front teeth. Apparently, when your parents had money, you could have early orthodontic treatment. "But first, I need to know who saw Paige Wentworth after lunch."

Several of the girls mentioned her last group dance. Others said she'd been with them on the way to the dressing room. Or at least they thought she was. "Wait," Jayne said, "is her coat here?" When no one moved, she asked Cindy to show her Paige's belongings.

In a smooth move that marked her as a strong dancer, Cindy transitioned from sitting with her legs crossed to standing position without putting a hand on the floor. Once upon a time, Jayne had been able to do that. Cindy went through Paige's things that were piled near hers. "I don't see her coat."

Jayne's heart sunk. "What exactly did she say before she left?"

Cindy shrugged, averting her gaze. Was she hiding something? Jayne could feel Cindy's mother watching them both. She'd have to catch Cindy alone. Maybe the girl would open up then.

Jayne shoved Paige out of her mind for a minute. The girl was sixteen, not a lost five-year-old. Jayne checked to make sure each dancer had a chaperone and a room to stay for the night. Three of the dancers would stay in Hannah and Jayne's adjoining rooms.

Lucky them.

Trying to remain confident and calm in front of her girls, Jayne said, "I'll check if the hotel restaurant can make us pizzas around seven, okay? We can have a pizza party in the lobby." She felt a bit like a heel to be celebrating when Mr. Diamond had died and Paige was missing, but she had to maintain some normalcy for the rest of the team.

"Why doesn't everyone pack up their costumes and use the tunnel to go to the hotel and get settled in your rooms? Meet in the lobby at seven?" She scanned the faces, then pointed to the moms. "No one walks alone. Stick to pairs. Younger dancers must stay with an adult chaperone."

Everyone nodded in agreement.

"My mom's still not here," a worried little dancer said, looking oddly more mature in her bright red lipstick and false eyelashes. Miss Natalie had often said she wasn't a fan of the makeup, but it was a component of competition dance, allowing their sweet faces to stand out on stage.

"I talked to the moms who went out for lunch. The restaurant across town is allowing them to stay until the roads clear."

The little girl's lip began to quiver and Jayne crouched down to get on the child's level. "She has all the breadsticks and soup she can eat. Sounds awesome, right?" Jayne's lips twitched as she forced a pleasant expression. Her heart broke for this little girl. "You like breadsticks, right?"

The girl nodded enthusiastically. "Tomatoes and olives are my favorites. The waitress brings me an entire plate of them if I say please."

"Lucky kid." Jayne squeezed the girl's hand. "How about a slumber party here at the hotel with your teammates? Fun, right?"

The little girl nodded again.

"It'll be an adventure."

"Okay," the child agreed, her voice growing a little stronger, despite the lingering uncertainty.

Jayne stood and her knees cracked. So much for having a dancer's body. Her mother appeared pale and tired under the unflattering fluorescent lighting. "Let's all take an afternoon break. We'll meet in the lobby hotel for pizza at seven."

Jayne wished she could go for a nap and wake up in her own bed on Monday because this weekend was stretching on forever.

CHAPTER SEVENTEEN

Jayne's mother sat on the edge of the bed with her ankles crossed, staring at the classic movie playing on the hotel TV. Her mother's level of fitness and smooth skin make her appear far younger than she was. She certainly didn't look like someone who was gradually succumbing to the horrible grip of Alzheimer's Disease. Hannah was sitting on the other queen bed, scrolling through her phone. Jayne plopped down next to her and almost jumped back up and started pacing. Her entire body felt like it was on a spring. She had a million worries bouncing around her head.

She leaned over and watched Hannah scroll through Paige's social media. "Has she posted anything in the past hour?" After the dancers from Murphy's Dance Academy vacated the dressing room, Cindy had caught up with Jayne and confided in her that Paige had gone out for coffee not just with some boy, but some boy she met on social media. This was so much worse than if it had been a boyfriend. Paige had left her phone behind because her mother often tracked it. All a great plan until someone went missing. Jayne didn't give Cindy a hard time because ultimately, she had come forward with the truth.

Or at least, Jayne hoped she had. She could hardly blame the teen for holding back in front of her mother.

Jayne gave a quick call to Danny, to learn he had pulled over at a Tim Horton's in Niagara Falls due to poor visibility. He'd come back to the hotel and talk to Cindy. Maybe she knew something about her friend that she hadn't realized.

"No new posts on Paige's accounts," Hannah said. "But there's a guy." She tapped the screen. "This must be him." She moved her fingers apart to blow up the image. Paige's social media sites were private, but fortunately, at some point, she had accepted Hannah's follow request. They were, after all, both seniors at Tranquility High.

"Do you recognize him?" Jayne asked.

Hannah squinted. "No, he doesn't go to our high school." If he had, Cindy would have known who he was. She would have said as much, right?

"Is that something you girls do? Hook up with guys on the Internet?" Jayne asked. Sure, her peers used dating apps, but why would a seventeen-year-old resort to that? They had plenty of opportunities to meet dates in school, unlike later in life when their worlds got smaller and smaller, with fewer and fewer prospects.

Hannah shrugged. "Not my scene, but I guess some teens do. I figure I might meet someone in college. Or at my first job." She held up her palms. "I'm in no hurry. Seems to be mostly a hassle." She shot Jayne a knowing glance.

Jayne scratched her chin. "Well, I guess it's better than thinking she disappeared into thin air. We know she left with someone. Now, we have to pray her date isn't an axe murderer." Jayne kept her voice low so as not to disrupt the movie for her mother. Miss Natalie had moved to the head of the bed and was relaxing against the pillows.

"Are you going to let Mrs. Wentworth know Paige is missing?" Hannah asked.

"After I talk to Danny. I'd only worry her, and there's not much she can do in this storm." Jayne didn't want to be responsible for her driving here in a panic and risk getting in an accident.

Yes, she thought to herself. Better to let it be. For another hour. If Paige didn't show up by then, she'd call the teen's parents.

Jayne pushed off the bed and snagged her cell phone from the desk. "I need to make a few calls. You mind hanging here with Miss Natalie?"

"My pleasure." Hannah scooted to the top of the bed and adjusted the pillows behind her. "Go, we'll be fine."

Jayne brushed a kiss across her mother's cheek before slipping out of the hotel room. She debated sitting in the hall to make her calls but decided the lobby would be more private. Who knew when one of the dancers might pop up in the hallway on their way to the vending machine or one of the other rooms? Instead, Jayne headed down the elevator to the lobby. She found a plush chair in a far corner away from curious ears and called Victoria Green. Their lives had become intertwined when the Greens moved into the house behind the Murphys' house. Jayne had to see how the grieving mother was doing after learning that someone had smashed her deceased daughter's bedroom window and that the person responsible for her daughter's death was out of jail. (For now.)

Deal with one issue at a time.

Mrs. Green answered on the third ring. "Hi Jayne," her neighbor said, sounding exhausted. "Officer Nolan told me you were out of town this weekend." What she didn't say but what was understood was, "Why are you calling me about the smashed window when you're busy with competition weekend?" Mrs. Green knew the business of dance competitions, having raised a dancer who'd planned on staking her claim in New York City.

Before she was run off the road and drowned.

"I wanted to check in. I have a little time because the competition got cancelled due to the weather."

"Oh, that's too bad," Mrs. Green said, not sounding particularly concerned one way or another.

Jayne wondered if calling Mrs. Green had been a mistake. Perhaps it brought up too many painful memories. She cleared her throat, suddenly feeling awkward. "How's the weather?" It seemed like a logical thing to ask someone who had moved to the Sunshine State.

"It's Florida. It rains for a few minutes, then it's sunny again." Mrs. Green seemed bored, or maybe she had taken tranquilizers. Losing her daughter had nearly destroyed her.

"I could use some sun. It's been snowing nonstop."

"Superstar Dance Power. Hmmm..." Mrs. Green said, seemingly lost in a memory. "I always loved that venue. Hard to believe that part of my life is over."

Jayne pressed her lips together and avoided saying something trite like, "It does go fast," or "Time flies." Mrs. Green didn't need to hear that. It was far more than the passing of time. She had lost her daughter forever.

"I'll be happy to be rid of that house," Mrs. Green said, apparently jumping back to the broken window conversation. The pain in Mrs. Green's voice was palpable.

Jayne felt a pang of regret mixed with hurt. This felt personal. They'd no longer be neighbors. But their relationship hadn't been the same since Melinda died. "You'll be missed," Jayne finally said.

"I'm not sure how comfortable I'd be back there now that I know Carol Anne was sleeping in Melinda's bed."

"What?" The single word came out as a squeak. Jayne

leaned forward and ran a hand across her forehead. "Carol Anne was in the house?" Now she understood why Danny was so quick to change the subject after telling her that Carol Anne had been released.

"*Someone* was in the house. Your police friend told me that the bed wasn't made. There were food wrappers on my daughter's nightstand..." Her voice cracked. "Who else could it be?"

Panic rose with the bile in the back of Jayne's throat. "I'm so sorry. That's awful." Jayne bit back the barrage of questions pinging around her head. Mrs. Green didn't need to rehash it on her account. She'd save the questions and her wrath for Danny. Did he think she wouldn't be able to handle the news? Why had he only told her part of the story?

A realization washed over her. He'd come to Niagara Falls to make sure she was safe with Carol Anne on the loose. Should she fault him for that? Wasn't it sweet? But why not tell her? Hadn't she felt like someone had been watching her? Something she had been willing to write off as paranoia.

When the silence stretched a beat too long, Jayne said, "I'll keep an eye on the house once I'm back home. Please put this out of your mind."

Mrs. Green exhaled a long sigh. "Thank you, dear. It's only a house. Be careful if that girl is around. She's not well."

A *beep-beep* sounded over the phone and Jayne saw a New York City area code appear on the screen. It might be spam, but it was a good excuse to wrap up the call.

"Anything you need, you know how to reach me."

"I know. Night, dear. Good luck at the competition."

Jayne didn't bother reminding her that the event had been canceled. What did it matter?

"Thanks. Good night." Jayne quickly clicked over to the other call. "Hello."

"Jayne? Jayne Murphy?" a woman asked, her tone hesitant.

Jayne found herself analyzing the voice, trying to make the quick decision if she should say she wasn't around—in the case that this was a dumb extended car warranty scam call—or if she should acknowledge they had reached their intended party. There was too much going on to risk it. "Yes, speaking."

"Jayne, this is Lola Diamond." Dale's daughter.

"Oh, Lola, I'm so sorry about your dad." *Darn it, she had meant to call the young woman.*

"Yeah..." She sniffed. "I'm trying get home, but all the flights are grounded because of the storm." Lola's brittle tone bordered on hysteria. "I can't believe he's gone."

"Who notified you?" Jayne's heartbeat thrummed in her ears. She knew all too well how it felt to learn of a sudden death of a loved one. It was brutal.

"The police." Jayne could imagine Lola clicking through her phone apps to find where she had taken a note of the officer's name. "Officer Fiorella. I wanted to ask him more questions, but I didn't write down his number."

Jayne recalled the short, stocky officer who seemed to be on a power trip shoving her into the elevator, then outside to his patrol car, but Lola wouldn't be interested in her drama. Jayne finally found her voice. "Danny might have his contact information."

"Danny?"

Jayne immediately realized her mistake. If she hoped to not get involved with this case, asking Danny for information to share with Lola was exactly the opposite of not getting involved. "Officer Danny Nolan from the Tranquility Police Department. He's a friend of mine. He showed up when the local police were here. He and Officer Fiorella were in the police academy together."

"Maybe he can talk to him for me. They say my dad was drunk. He doesn't drink." Disbelief laced Lola's tone.

A heavy weight pressed on Jayne's chest making it difficult to draw in a deep breath. Right at this very minute, she felt like she had a million balls she was trying to juggle. And was it appropriate to tell Lola that she had found her father's body along with housekeeping? And that he had been drunk? She had seen him throwing back drinks in the casino. It would break Lola's heart.

"I'm here for whatever you need," Jayne said, part of her trait of not being able to say no. Her mind raced. "When was the last time you talked to your dad?" She expected to hear some lament about how she hadn't talked to him in weeks, and had meant to call, and how she had been busy. Excuses. Everyone had them when they learned about someone's sudden passing and the guilt started to settle in.

Instead, Lola said, "Last night."

A jolt zinged through Jayne's nervous system. "You spoke to him *last night?*" Hadn't she noticed his slurred speech? "What time?"

"Around midnight."

"Do you usually talk to your dad that late?"

"He called me. He does that sometimes. He knows I'm an insomniac."

Jayne's investigative instincts made her scalp prickle. "Do you mind if I ask what you talked about?"

"The usual. Auditions I went on." Lola sniffed. "I got a callback for an off-Broadway show." Now the joyous occasion had turned melancholy.

"How did he seem?" Jayne tiptoed around what she really wanted to ask. Mr. Diamond had been three sheets to the wind when she saw him at the casino last night. It lined up with the story that he had fallen and hit his head.

"Fine. Tired maybe." Lola sighed. "He wasn't drunk. I was about to tell him about my callback when someone knocked on the door."

Someone was there? Someone came to visit Mr. Diamond?

Adrenaline surged through Jayne's veins. "Who was it?"

"I don't know. He said he had to go and hurriedly ended the call." A sob sounded over the line. "And that was the last time I'll ever talk to my dad."

"I'm so sorry, Lola. I really am."

"Me too." Lola's ragged breathing sounded over the line. "I'd appreciate it if you could get more information for me. I have no idea when I'll be able to get a flight out of here."

"I'll do what I can." A nagging helplessness washed over her. "Take care, Lola."

"Thanks, Jayne."

She was about to hang up when she heard the grieving daughter mutter something that sounded like, "What a nightmare."

CHAPTER EIGHTEEN

After Jayne ended the call with Lola Diamond, she paced the lobby. Outside the windows, the wind and snow swirled. She pulled the two sides of her hoodie together and stifled a shudder. It was only late afternoon, but it felt much later.

Dale Diamond.
Paige Wentworth.
Carol Anne Green.

Too many things bouncing around her brain and she was stuck here in this hotel because of the weather. Even if she tried to be the hero and go out in the storm to find Paige, she'd end up being the next person local law enforcement had to save, and she didn't want to be that person. She already had a lot of officers looking down their noses at her because she was what they called a "wannabe cop."

Drumming her fingers on her thigh, she realized she wasn't reaching out to one of the resources at her disposal. She scrolled through her contacts and held her breath while the phone rang. Teddy Wysocki answered the phone on the third ring.

"Hi Teddy, it's Jayne." The private investigator she was training under didn't believe in caller ID or cell phones, so she should consider herself lucky that he answered the phone at all. However, he did live in the back of the squat, one-story brick building that housed Wysocki and Sons' Investigations. (He also didn't have any sons.)

"It's really coming down out there, isn't it?" Teddy said, seemly unhurried and not particularly curious as to why she called.

Jayne turned her back to the large window overlooking the cobblestone street in a rehabilitated section of Niagara Falls. Yes, it was coming down, both here and thirty minutes away in Tranquility.

"I hope you're not out on a case tonight," he continued, his voice gruff from years of cigarettes and probably because she'd woken him from a pre-dinner nap. She could imagine him smoothing a hand over his unruly hair.

"Not intentionally." She hugged her arms around her midsection, trying to decide where to start. *Paige. Definitely Paige.* "I'm in Niagara Falls at a dance competition."

"I didn't know you danced," he said, deadpan. Jayne didn't bother correcting him, because she knew he was joking. At least, she was 99% certain he was kidding. "I hope you don't have to drive in this. Your old beater will end up in a ditch. You better not be calling me from a ditch because I don't have a truck to be pulling people out of ditches."

"I'm not in a ditch." Not a literal one, anyway. "I'm hunkered down at a hotel."

"I must be paying you too much."

"Ha," Jayne said. "At least I'm not asking you to get me out of a ditch." A beat of silence stretched between them. "I have a few things going on here."

The squeak his office chair made sounded over the line, as

if he were leaning forward to grab his pen, the cap chewed. "Whatcha got?"

"It's like the world is coming to an end." An all too familiar icy dread pooled in her gut. "Hey, did you know Carol Anne isn't in custody anymore?" she blurted out even though she fully intended on focusing on finding Paige first.

"Carol Anne goes by the last name Green, right?" He probably wrote her name in his tight, illegible handwriting on a yellowing telephone message pad. "Want me to see where she's staying?"

"Maybe." The thought of Creepy Carol—as the kids in elementary school used to call her—wandering around free was unnerving to say the least, but she wasn't the top priority. *And why hadn't Danny told her she was hunkering down in the Greens' house?* "My first priority is one of my dancers who is missing."

"You call the local police?" Teddy asked, sounding perplexed.

"It's not like that." Or at least, she prayed it wasn't. "She's sixteen, and one of her friends thinks she met a guy for coffee. They're probably snowed in somewhere. I have a screenshot of one of his socials. I'll e-mail it to you. Can you do a little digging, reassure me he's not a stalker?"

"I can see what I can find online." Teddy had a lot of tools at his disposal. He'd probably find this kid's home address in five minutes. "At least I can still do that in this storm."

"I'd appreciate it."

"Jayne, maybe you should have local PD search for her and her guy friend. I'd do it myself but..."

"Yeah, the storm." She glanced toward the windows. The snow wasn't showing any signs of letting up. "I have one more thing for you."

"Sure." Teddy sounded pleased, as if this phone call was the most exciting thing in his day.

"I found a dead body this morning."

Her mentor sputtered. "Um, I think you buried the lede." He was probably shaking his head. "Have I taught you nothing?"

Jayne absentmindedly wandered over to a leather chair and plopped into it. "Yeah, it might have been an accident, but it didn't feel right to me." She lifted her gaze and glanced around, realizing she had been so deep in her own head that she hadn't made sure no one was listening. "Can you do some digging on Dale Diamond? See if he has any huge debt. I found him at the casino last night drunk and bemoaning the fact that he was being forced out as emcee of Superstar Dance Power. There had been accusations about his behavior too." Jayne told Teddy all the details she had surrounding Dale Diamond and his death. "I know his daughter from her years dancing. I hope to give her some answers."

"The funny thing about family seeking answers, they think losing their loved one was hard...until they learn the truth about their death."

"Not knowing is worse," Jayne said, rubbing her forehead. She remembered all the opinion pieces in the local paper speculating about how her brother died in the line of duty. "I'd like to find answers, but I'm not even sure where to start. Being stuck at the hotel isn't helping."

"Did you find any paying clients in all this?"

Jayne laughed even though nothing was funny. "No paying customers, but once people learn how smart we are, we'll be awash in cash from all the cases that will come our way."

Teddy guffawed. He had been at this far too long and wasn't nearly as enthusiastic as Jayne when it came to digging up information for the sake of the hunt. Goodwill didn't pay the bills.

"Okay, anything else on this Diamond guy?"

After Jayne repeated a few of the details surrounding Mr.

Diamond's death, she e-mailed Teddy the photo of the guy Paige had apparently gone for coffee with. She attached a photo of Paige too.

"Is that the daughter of the divorce case we worked?" Teddy asked.

"Yes."

"Oh man, I hate to see when the kids get messed up."

Jayne bristled at the comment. She didn't like to think of Paige as messed up. Determined. Independent. *But messed up?*

"She's young and made a dumb decision. If the weather wasn't bad, she probably would have snuck back into the competition and no one would have been the wiser."

"Yeah, kids never think of potential consequences. That's why I never had any kids."

Not to mention that he had never married, but she decided to keep her mouth shut.

"Okay, I'll start Googling," Teddy said, but Jayne knew he had far more effective resources than the average Internet user, like search engines that required passwords and payment and authorization. "I'll start with Paige Wentworth and her..." the clicking of keys on his keyboard sounded over the phone, "...and her debonaire dude."

Jayne glanced at the photo on her cell phone. He wasn't exactly Jayne's type, but to each their own. "Thanks, Teddy."

"You got it, kid."

Her heart warmed to him. He had the outer shell of a curmudgeon, but he was a softy inside. For some strange reason, it made her miss her dad. He'd never grow old and grumpy, not that he would have if he had lived. She bit her bottom lip to regain her composure.

"Hey, one more thing, Teddy. See if you can find anything on an Amber Mack. She's mid-twenties and works for Superstar Dance Power."

"Oh?" Teddy sounded intrigued. "How is she involved in all of this?"

"I'm not sure. Mr. Diamond was worried about being replaced by her and he asked me to dig up anything I could. I hadn't accepted the job before he died."

"You're determined to work for free, aren't you?" Teddy's tone held a hint of humor.

"Can't collect from a dead guy," Jayne returned his banter.

"Very true." He cleared his throat. "I'll call you when I find something."

"Thanks, Teddy. Night."

She ended the call and turned around to find Cindy standing a few feet away, apparently waiting for Jayne to get off the phone. She looked pale and her eyes were wide with fear. *How long had she been standing there?*

"Hi, Cindy." Jayne narrowed her gaze. "What's wrong? Did you hear from Paige?"

Cindy nodded, and a tear rolled down her cheek.

Jayne wrapped her arm around the distraught young woman. "Tell me." Jayne found her own panic growing.

Cindy drew in a shuddering breath and held up her cell phone. "Paige texted me."

Jayne took the phone and studied the screen. It was the image of a license plate. "How did she send this? We have her phone."

"I don't know. All I got was this photo and the text, 'If something happens to me. LOL.'"

Cindy was far from LOL'ing.

CHAPTER NINETEEN

Danny wondered if he hadn't stopped to grab a coffee and donut at Tim Horton's in Niagara Falls if he would have been home already and not stuck in this slow-moving line of traffic headed toward the expressway. Or maybe he'd be stuck *on* the expressway which would be worse. Initially, he had thoughts of waiting out the storm in the coffee shop, but his impatience had gotten the best of him.

He had come to Niagara Falls to tell Jayne firsthand about Carol Anne. If the unhinged woman had been sleeping in her stepsister's bed across the yard from Jayne's house, he wanted to make sure Jayne was safe. However with the storm, he realized Carol Anne probably wouldn't have the mobility to harass Jayne, so he had decided to head back to Tranquility. But now, that didn't see like such a good idea either.

The wiper blades skidded over icy chunks that clung to his windshield. A knot formed in his lower back as he held the steering wheel in a death grip. Maybe he should take surface roads instead. The screen on the dash lit up with an incoming call. *Jayne.* He clicked accept and looked up at the exact moment a car veered into his lane. He jerked the steering wheel to the right, and the car bearing down on him swerved back into the opposite lane, avoiding sideswiping him.

"Hey!" He gestured angrily with his hand. "Darn it. Jerk!" His anger trumped his fear. What a close call!

"Um, Danny, it's Jayne."

He dragged his hand through his hair. "Sorry, sorry. These roads are awful. People forget how to drive when it snows."

She sighed heavily. "I shouldn't have called you. You're driving in this weather..."

"I'm fine. Hands free and all. Tell me what's wrong." He glanced into his side mirror and pulled off the road into a gas station parking lot.

"I'm worried about Paige Wentworth. She left the convention center with some boy she met online."

Danny groaned. He wasn't much older, but this next crop of kids seemed to think nothing of meeting people in real life that they initially met online. When he was in middle school, the administration had constantly brought in experts to scare the assembled kids about the dangers of the Internet. It seemed parents, teachers, and faculty were baffled by the explosion of social media. Handwritten notes passed between earlier generations of students had turned into mean-spirited texts or public posts for the whole world to consume. It was a tough way to grow up, but it was the only thing these kids knew. People they met online were considered friends. The dangers had been forgotten.

It didn't mean they didn't exist.

"I'm still in Niagara Falls," Danny said. "What information do you have on her location?"

"Thank goodness," Jayne breathed out in barely a whisper, obviously relieved that he was still in town. "I have his license plate."

"Good. I can get a name and address from that."

"Teddy's doing a search on this guy for me too. If he comes up with anything, I'll give you a heads up."

"I'd appreciate it. I'll be in touch." Danny hung up, then called one of his peers on duty. Turned out Paige's mystery man had a clean record, but it didn't mean he had innocent intentions. Lots of jerks hadn't been caught yet. He hoped for Paige's sake, he was just a good guy who'd had a bad idea.

Jayne hated having more questions than answers, especially while trapped at the hotel. She'd have to be content knowing Danny and Teddy were using their resources to track Paige down. That would have to do. For now.

Jayne took the elevator up and found a few of the girls gathered in Hannah's room watching a Disney movie with their beloved Miss Natalie. Her mother was leaning against the pillows dozing.

Hannah was sitting in a chair near the adjoining door. She stood and tipped her chin toward the TV screen, indicating everyone was occupied. She joined Jayne in her room. Keeping her voice low, Hannah asked, "Any word on Paige?"

Jayne reflexively checked the cell phone in her hand. "Not yet." She cut her friend a sideways glance. "Why would she take that risk and meet a stranger?"

Hannah shrugged. Paige was the product of a very messy divorce. Undoubtedly, attention was attention, regardless of how she got it.

"*You* better not do something like that," Jayne whispered, raising her eyebrows.

Hannah laughed. "Are you kidding? I watch far too many true crime stories to fall for that nonsense. I'm not going to end up being in some online news story where jerks make rude comments about what an idiot I was."

Jayne would have laughed, except for the image she couldn't shake: that of Paige Wentworth's pretty face plastered on the local newspaper—in her case, on the front page, above the fold: *Daughter of well-known lawyer, Harrison Wentworth, has been found beaten to death at a man's house. She met the man...*

Jayne visibly shuddered. Now was not the time to allow her active imagination to get away from her. Paige was going to be fine. Embarrassed. Disciplined. But okay. In the other room, someone's cellphone rang. None of the girls bothered to check their phones. Curious, Jayne followed the sound and stopped at Paige's things, which Cindy had rolled here for safekeeping.

Jayne crouched down, digging into the bag and plucking out Paige's phone. A photo of Paige and her mother flashed on the screen. Jayne's shoulders sagged. She swiped her finger across the screen, then met Hannah's gaze—a silent understanding traveling between them. Jayne returned to her room before saying, "Hello." An uneasiness made her knees wobbly.

"Paige!" Tiffany Wentworth shouted, her voice a mix between panicked and outright annoyance. "Why haven't you answered your phone? I've been trying to reach you all—"

"Mrs. Wentworth," Jayne interrupted her. "It's Jayne."

"Why are you answering my daughter's phone?" The edge to her voice had softened into concern stemming from the confusion of someone unexpected picking up their teen's phone. "Jayne, please put on Paige." Mrs. Wentworth's tone was terse.

"Paige isn't here." Jayne hated how her voice squeaked on the word, "here."

"Where is she?" The woman's voice grew haughty, a tone Jayne had been accustomed to until she had gotten to know the timid woman behind the cool exterior. A woman who had been humbled when she'd learned her husband was cheating on her. When she realized she'd be left with nothing after her divorce if she didn't have proof of his infidelity, Tiffany Wentworth had been Jayne's first paying client. For that reason alone, Jayne would give this woman a pass. Jayne would forgive Mrs. Wentworth for being rude because she was worried about her daughter.

Heck, Jayne was worried about Paige, too, and she probably should have called her mom before now, but she had thought Paige would have returned before Jayne was forced to make that call.

"I don't know where Paige is."

"You don't—"

"Please, hear me out."

Jayne gave Paige's mother the rundown of the day's events. She debated whether she was continuing the deceit by sugarcoating everything. Did the woman really need to know her daughter had texted her friend a just-in-case photo of her date's license plate?

"My friend, Danny Nolan, is tracking her down. They were able to figure out who she was with."

"Who was she with?"

"I honestly don't know his name. But Danny is going to call me as soon as he knows more." Jayne rubbed her forehead, another headache forming behind her eyes.

Silence stretched across the line. Jayne racked her brain on how she was going to reassure this mom that everything was going to be okay.

Mrs. Wentworth broke the silence. "Call me as soon as you hear from Officer Nolan."

"I will, I will."

"Please don't call her father. You know how he is."

Jayne did know. She had seen the scary side of Harrison Wentworth when he'd low-key threatened her after he discovered she was tailing him. When Mr. Wentworth showed up at the studio, she had decided right then and there that she shouldn't take cases that overlapped with her real life, and especially ones that involved dancers or their families.

"I'll call you as soon as I get word of where she is." Jayne cleared her throat. "And I'm sorry. This should have never happened."

"Paige is a big girl. She would have found a way to do it somehow. She's been breaking curfew and getting on my last nerve. She's begging for attention. Between the divorce and all her little brother's activities, it's exhausting. She's fine." The word "fine" came out on a long sigh, as if the woman wasn't too concerned, or was too tired to care. And therein was the problem.

"I can imagine." Jayne decided she'd roll with it. Better to have Paige's mom acknowledging her daughter had to take responsibility for her own actions. But real relief wouldn't come until the young woman was back at the hotel, safe and sound. "I'll call you as soon as I talk to Paige."

"Thanks, Jayne. Hey!" Mrs. Wentworth shouted at someone at her end. "Stop bouncing a ball in the house! Now!"

Jayne pulled the phone away from her ear and winced, the woman's shrill voice scraping across her brain.

"Sorry, I have to stop this kid. I'm too old for this," she muttered. "Way too old."

Jayne ended the call, then leaned against the wall in her hotel room. A door slammed somewhere on their floor. She opened the door and looked down the hall, one way, then another. A red blinking light high up near the ceiling caught her attention. A camera. If there was a camera on this floor, there was probably one on every floor. Including Dale Diamond's. Had it captured the person who came to his door last night when Lola was talking to her dad?

She slipped back into the adjoining room and found Hannah waiting near the door. "You got this?"

"Of course."

"Hey, I have pizza coming to the lobby at seven from the hotel restaurant. Don't forget to go down. I'm sure you're hungry."

"Food!" Hannah said, waggling her eyebrows. "I'll be there."

"Thanks." Jayne gently touched Hannah's wrist. "I'll try to meet you there. I need to check something out." She left the room, amazed that Hannah and Paige were the same age. Jayne could never imagine Hannah doing something so boneheaded as meeting a stranger during a dance competition and leaving everyone worried to death.

CHAPTER TWENTY

Lola Diamond's words rose above the din of things demanding Jayne's attention: "Someone came to my father's door." Was Mr. Diamond's death truly an accident, or had this late-night visitor been responsible? Mr. Diamond's scuffed shoes came to mind. It might be a stretch, but she sensed it meant something. The man had been meticulous in dress, including his polished shoes.

Curiosity killed the cat.

Jayne took the elevator down to the lobby and across to the reception desk. A man sat there drumming a pen on the desk and holding up his head with his fist. She was surprised he wasn't on his cell phone. A twinge prickled the back of her neck. He probably had strict instructions not to use his phone during work hours. If the clerk was a rule follower when no one was around, she probably wouldn't be able to talk him into helping her with something that was certainly against hotel policy.

When he saw her, he straightened and shuffled behind the computer monitor, ready to serve. "Good afternoon, ma'am. May I help you?"

Jayne rested her forearms on the desk and smiled. "It's pretty quiet around here." She glanced at his name tag: *Freddie*.

The kid shrugged. "Weather doesn't help."

"How'd you get to work with all the snow?" Jayne pivoted to glance toward the wall of windows overlooking the snowy street.

"I don't live far. And I got a truck. That beast is amazing in snow." He puffed up his chest, then laughed ruefully. "My boss knows that too. Otherwise I would have called in like everyone else." He shook his head, apparently sensing that he was going on too long. "Sorry, what can I help you with?"

A bubble of hope warmed her belly. Maybe Freddie was the right amount of bored and annoyed at "the man" to do her a favor. "I imagine you heard about the gentleman who died in room 1997 last night?"

One brow drew down and he narrowed his gaze at her, probably wondering how she knew the exact room where Mr. Diamond had died. "Yeah, I guess I should be glad I don't work in housekeeping, huh?" He made a dramatic shudder, then met her gaze. "Oh sorry, was he a friend of yours?"

"I've known Mr. Diamond for a long time. I know his daughter too. She's a dancer and she's stuck in New York City." Jayne clasped her hands together and rested them on the counter in front of her. "She told me her father answered the door to someone shortly before he died."

He ran a hand across his forehead. "Oh. I thought it was an accident. Dude...I mean, the gentleman was drunk. Fell and knocked himself out."

"Oh, I'm not saying the person hurt Mr. Diamond. I'd like to talk to them. That's all. See if he seemed okay before he passed." She paused long enough for dramatic effect. "Sad, isn't it? His daughter would take comfort in talking to the person who saw him last." She pressed her lips together. "I see the hotel has cameras on each floor. Do you have access to them?"

The kid rocked back on his heels. "Yeah, no. I mean, I don't want to lose my job."

"Who would know?" Jayne made a big show of looking one way, then another, emphasizing the empty lobby. "I won't take long. I need to see floor nineteen from last night."

"I don't think so."

"It wouldn't take long. I can narrow it down to a short timeframe. Jayne pulled out her phone and texted Lola. "What time did you talk to your dad last night?"

The bubbles appeared immediately. *Ten forty-five.*

Jayne glanced up. "I need to see ten-thirty to eleven. I'll speed up the playback. It'll take no time at all." She dug into her back pocket and slid a fifty-dollar bill across the counter.

A corner of Freddie's mouth twitched. The kid wanted this money as much as she wanted to see the camera feed.

"No one will know," she coaxed. "And you'd be doing his distraught daughter a real favor."

"My dad died two years ago from cancer," Freddie said, almost to himself.

"I'm sorry," Jayne said. "That's hard." She didn't mention her own father's passing because that felt like she'd be laying it on too thick.

The kid's shoulders sagged, indicating he was folding like a card table at a Buffalo Bills' tailgate party. And sure enough, he pocked the money and stepped out from behind the computer. "Okay, come on." He tilted his head toward the back room. Jayne followed him. Three monitors sat above a keyboard. A black and white view of the lobby flipped over to the view of a stark, cement stairwell, then to a corridor. Each monitor scrolled through various locations. The kid held up his hand. "It's recording on all the cameras." He pulled out a chair and flopped down. He typed in a few things on the keypad. "It stores the files in the cloud." He clicked a few more keys. "The nineteenth floor, right?"

"Yes." Her heart raced. She was so close to possibly getting an answer. "Between ten and eleven last night."

Freddie dragged the cursor along the bottom of the middle screen and people came and went at rapid succession. Then, when the numbers on the bottom of the monitor read 10:52, a shadowy figure appeared.

Jayne pointed. "Stop. Stop there." The kid hit pause, then play and the scene unfolded at normal speed. Someone dressed in black stopped at what could have been Dale Diamond's door. She squinted and leaned closer to the monitor, trying to make out a face, but the person had on a hood and stayed turned away from the cameras, as if they knew they were there. As if they had gone there for nefarious reasons. "Is there a way to zoom in?"

"Hold up." The kid tried a few more keystrokes. The image got bigger but it also got grainier. The resolution was horrible.

"Stop there." Jayne took a photo of the still frame on her cell phone, not very confident that it would be of use. "Okay."

The kid hit play and the shadow disappeared into the room.

They watched in silence. No one came or went for ten minutes. The figure emerged from the room and strolled away. Still no way to ID them.

"Can you pull up the cameras on the elevators?" She held her breath.

The kid clicked through all the views of the elevators for the period after the person left Dale's room. "Nothing."

"What about the stairwells?"

The kids sighed and clicked a few more keys. Apparently,

the respite from his boredom at the counter hadn't turned out to be that much fun.

"Hello? Hello?" a female's voice floated back to them from the front desk. "Um, is anyone working?"

Freddie pushed back from the monitor and stood. "Sorry, I gotta get this." For a heartbeat, she considered sitting at the desk and resuming the search where Freddie had left off but he had been on to her. "You've got to leave. I don't want to get fired."

"Did the police ask to see these?" Jayne asked.

Freddie shrugged. "Not while I was here. But maybe Parson will know. He was working earlier."

"Can you text him and ask?"

Freddie held up a finger. He went out front and Jayne followed. An older woman stood at the desk with a look of complete exasperation on her face. "It's about time," she said curtly, her eyes going from the kid to Jayne and back.

Jayne was too lost in her thoughts to be embarrassed by the implication in the woman's big-eyed stare.

Jayne sat down on a chair near the front desk and waited. After the woman left, Freddie walked over with his phone in hand. "Parson said no one asked to see the feed. He also said he overhead the police say it was an accidental death."

Jayne pushed to a standing position. "Okay, thanks."

"Good thing it wasn't something else," Freddie said.

"What do you mean, 'something else'?"

Freddie slid behind the desk and leaned his forearms on the counter. "Business took a tank after the last death." He cut his gaze left, then right. Jayne expected him to mention the old lady that Garrett in housekeeping had told her about. She really needed to do some research and see how many people died of natural causes per year in hotels. It only made sense that it would be "a lot."

Freddie continued, "We had a rash of drug ODs here last

fall. People began calling this place 'Hotel California.' You know, you can't leave after you check in, or something like that. Some really old song."

Jayne found herself narrowing her gaze, intrigued by the teen's choice in music. Or maybe he was simply repeating something he had heard. Anyway, that wasn't the point. "Mr. Diamond wasn't into drugs." As far as she knew.

"A death is a death. The hotel has been taking a beating." As if on a cue, a couple young dancers ran across the lobby and ducked into the vending machine alcove. "You think all these people gonna want to bring their daughters here for a convention with drug dealers around? People being murdered in their rooms? I overheard my boss. The police want this to go away quietly, and so does the hotel."

Jayne patted the desk with her open palm. "Thanks for the info."

Freddie's face flushed red. "Don't tell anyone I let you look at the cameras. This is a boring job, but I get paid extra for working these craptastic shifts."

"I won't," Jayne said, but it didn't mean she wasn't going to follow up on what she saw on the video feeds.

CHAPTER TWENTY-ONE

The snow crunched under Danny's tires as he drove slowly down the residential street. He'd gotten the address of Paige Wentworth's mystery man from his vehicle registration, thanks to the plate numbers. One of his fellow officers in Tranquility had sent him a screenshot of the guy's license. Old, unshaven, with an evil look in his eye. Or maybe Danny was just thinking the worst. He didn't want to consider why an old man would be talking to a young girl on the Internet.

Damn Internet. His brain searched for the term for this. Ah, catfishing. But that didn't explain why Paige would climb into the guy's truck once he showed up. Now way. It would have to be a much bigger ruse.

Oh, Paige. Sometimes Danny hated people. They had endless creative ways to hurt and deceive people.

Pulse roaring in his ears, he pulled into the narrow driveway behind a pickup truck. It got dark early at this time of the year. His headlights lit on the license plate before he cut the engine. Right truck, now he had to hope Paige was inside. He wanted to catch this guy by surprise if he could.

Danny zipped up his coat and climbed out of the truck. His boots sunk into the freshly fallen snow. *Ugh.* It had been a few years since they had a storm of this magnitude. He blinked against the large, wet snowflakes. Didn't seem like it was going to taper off anytime soon.

Danny scanned the facade of the two-story house. In the dark—and if he squinted a little—it was reminiscent of the great homes in Niagara Falls before time and poverty wore away at them. Deep porches graced both stories, common for this era home. Neighbors used to sit outside and chat pre-central air. Now, the outside living space served as storage space for snow-covered bikes, Christmas decorations, and rusted grills. Most of these homes had two separate units, and one family lived upstairs, the other down. He wondered which floor Romeo occupied. His gaze followed tracks in the snow, partially covered by snowdrifts, that led up to the front porch of the first floor.

Danny glanced around. He went around to the passenger side and grabbed his personal firearm from the glovebox and fixed the holster on his belt. Not a soul was out. The blanket of snow gave the street an otherworldly feel. Still. Clean. Renewed.

Danny climbed the steps, skirted the bike leaning against the railing, and peered into the cloudy window created from a broken seal, probably a long time ago. A narrow crack between heavy blinds revealed the flickering light from a TV. From this angle, he couldn't see anything else. He backed up and went around to the door. He lifted his hand and knocked. A clump of snow fell from the overhang and landed on his shoulder.

"Man, I hate winter," he muttered.

A minute later, a young man who did not match the photo on the license Danny had seen came to the door, glancing at something in his hand. Money?

The man opened the door, counted off a few bills, then narrowed his gaze at Danny in confusion. "How much..." His voice trailed off, seeing that the person standing on his porch was not from whatever app he had used to order food. The man's demeanor changed and he planted his hand on the door, as if he were about to slam it shut.

Danny opened the storm door with black metal bars and quickly put his foot in the doorframe. "Security door only works when you remember to lock it," Danny said, giving off alpha dog vibes, then he asked, "Is this your truck in the driveway?"

The man narrowed his gaze with a what's-it-to-you vibe.

"It is your truck?" Danny repeated with an edge to his tone.

"Yeah, I mean, it's my uncle's but he lets me take it whenever I want."

"Okay, then you're the guy I'm looking for."

The man smirked, "What do you want?"

"I'm looking for a friend of mine. Paige?" Danny studied the guy's face.

"Oh..." His faux rage at being disturbed melted away and his jaw grew slack. "I was going to give her a ride back once the snow stopped."

"I'm her ride."

The man ran a hand across his brow. "Oh." He turned and hollered over his shoulder, "Paige, some guy's here for you."

A moment later, Paige peered around the corner. The bare bulb on a sconce revealed a wariness in her eyes. But recognition made her smile. "Hi, Danny!" she said. "Let me get my jacket." She disappeared, then reappeared a minute later. She raised her hand in a quick goodbye, slid by the guy who'd answered the door, and joined Danny on the porch. "Let's go."

He followed her to his truck and they both climbed in.

"Thank goodness. I was getting so bored. That guy only watches the History Channel."

Danny started the vehicle, turned on the heat, then shifted to look at his passenger. "Are you okay? Did he hurt you?"

"Hurt me? No. Unless you call being bored to death a capital offense." Paige seemed blissfully unaware of the drama she had caused by disappearing from the dance competition.

"Are you sure you're okay?" He didn't know how many more ways he could ask. But based on her body language, she seemed fine, just annoyed that the date hadn't turned out as she had hoped.

"Yeah, fine. Bad date, that's all. How'd you find me?"

"The license plate photo you sent."

Paige chuckled and tapped on her temple with her index finger. "Good thinking, right?"

"Paige, this isn't a game. Yes, it was smart that you let your friend know something about where you'd be, but you went off with a stranger you met on the Internet."

Paige smirked. "We've been talking for weeks. He's not a stranger."

"I'm going to disagree with you." He ran his palm over the top of the steering wheel. "You put Jayne Murphy in a horrible position. She's responsible for all the dancers from her studio. You have a lot of people worried about you." He put the truck into reverse, made sure the street was clear, and gunned it out of the snowy driveway. "Not cool, not cool at all."

Paige held out her hands in front of her. "Well here I am." Despite her chilly attitude, there was a hint of embarrassment in her tone.

Danny shook his head, then called Jayne over his truck Bluetooth. "Did you find her?" she asked without saying hello.

"Yes..." He cut a gaze over to Paige, who seemed to be studying her hands now. "She's right here. I'm bringing her back to the hotel. You're on speaker."

"Oh, thank goodness. Paige," Jayne said, "are you okay?"

"I'm fine," Paige said, exasperated. Danny didn't have a lot of experience with teen girls, but he recognized attitude when he saw it.

Apparently hearing it too, Jayne said in a clipped tone, "We were worried. I'll be waiting in the lobby. I'll talk to you then."

CHAPTER TWENTY-TWO

Jayne dialed Tiffany's number. *Paige's mother.* The call went straight to voicemail. *Odd, considering her daughter had been missing.* Jayne left a message that Paige was safe and on her way back to the hotel and to please call if she wanted to talk. Jayne apologized again for the chaos, hoping she wouldn't be hearing from Mr. Wentworth. He was an overbearing jerk—and a lawyer—who already didn't like her. Then she called Mrs. Peters, Cindy's mom, who assured her that Paige could stay in their hotel room tonight and that she would keep an eye on her. Mrs. Peters's tone suggested she'd do what Paige's own mother was incapable of doing.

Jayne hated these dynamics sometimes. Mother pitted against mother as if there was an award for being the best. Jayne also shot Hannah a quick text to give her an update.

Having seemingly solved one problem, Jayne collapsed into a plush chair in the lobby facing the windows. An uneasiness prickled the back of her neck and when she shifted around, she saw the desk clerk staring at her. Maybe Freddie was second-guessing his decision to let Jayne look at the security cams. She turned away from him. *Too late now.*

She had a grainy photos of probably the last person to see Mr. Diamond alive. Maybe now she could get the Niagara Falls police to investigate his death as more than an accident. Or, at the very least, get confirmation from the mystery person that Mr. Diamond had been okay when they left. Drunk, but okay.

Something felt very off about all of this. Or maybe she couldn't trust her intuition right now with everything that was going on in her life. Being stuck at a hotel in a snowstorm didn't help.

Just when she thought she couldn't possibly rehash the same thing in her head yet again, Danny and Paige came in through the glass doors, bringing in a draft of cold air and enormous relief.

Danny stomped his feet on the rug to shake off the snow. His strong presence radiated police officer vibes, something Jayne worried she'd never have—if she ever had a chance to return to the police academy. *If* she returned. Maybe this PI gig would be the way to go, giving her the flexibility to work the assignments she wanted, when she wanted, allowing her to be there for her mother and the dance studio.

"Welcome back!" Jayne rose and stopped short in front of Paige. Jayne was unable to keep the sarcasm out of her tone. Paige had her arms folded tightly in front of her and her head was slightly bowed, maybe contrite, or maybe freezing. The young woman certainly wasn't dressed for the weather. She must have thrown her fleece jacket on in a hurry, leaving her with only her sweatpants over her leotard, her feet tucked into fleece lined Ugg clogs.

No hat. No gloves. No boots.

Jayne shivered again, then pulled the reluctant young woman into a fierce hug, unable to hold a grudge. The teen smelled of cold air and cigarettes. Jayne made a split-second decision to let that go, hoping it was the "friend" who had partaken in the nasty habit, and not her. "Thank goodness you're okay," Jayne said.

Paige stiffened, then seemed to give up and melted into Jayne's embrace. Paige wrapped her arms around Jayne and squeezed. "I'm sorry." The young woman's words were muffled in Jayne's shoulder. "I was stupid. We were going to get coffee, but then the snow, and he said he lived close..." She pulled away and swiped a hand across her wet cheek. "So stupid," she repeated, then more quietly she added, "it was nice to have someone pay attention to me."

"Sweetie, you're not stupid. Please don't say that." Jayne tilted her head to meet her gaze. "You're a very smart woman, that's why I'm surprised you'd take such a dangerous risk."

Danny hung back, giving them room to talk. He probably had already given her an earful on how many ways meeting a stranger on the Internet could have gone wrong. So, so terribly wrong. With that thought, Jayne realized she didn't know that it hadn't.

"Are you okay? Did he hurt you?"

Paige laugh-cried and rolled her eyes, another tear tracking down her cheek. Her mascara streaked under one eye. "No, he didn't hurt me." She shook her head and stared at the ground. "He probably could have gotten back to the convention center, but he insisted with the snow that his apartment was closer. We watched some dumb history movie and he talked about video games. The guy had zero game, not that I wanted him to. I wanted to go back. I was worried about missing the competition. I *never* planned to be gone that long."

"You were smart to send Cindy the license plate number." Jayne wanted to give credit where credit was due. Without that information, Jayne would still be pacing the lobby and going out of her mind with worry.

"I would have been smarter to bring my phone." Paige

drew in a deep breath, then relaxed her shoulders. "But my mom checks my location. She trusts me about as much as she trusted my dad."

"I'm sorry." The poor teen had been through a lot with her parents' divorce.

"Yeah..." Paige let her voice trail off.

Danny approached and casually put his hand on Jayne's shoulder. Her belly did a little flip despite her determination to resist his charms. "Do I need to go and rough this guy up?" He raised an eyebrow, already knowing the answer.

"He can live to hook up online another day," Paige deadpanned.

Jayne held out her hand toward the bank of elevators. "I'll take you up to Cindy's room."

Paige laughed and hiccupped. "I can make it there on my own."

Jayne sucked in a breath, about to argue. Hadn't this been the same girl who had snuck out of the hotel unchecked? Paige must have read her mind because she quickly added, "Trust me, I learned my lesson. Besides, I miss my phone. Cindy has it."

Jayne laughed. "Okay. Sleep well."

"You too," Paige said. "And I'm sorry. I won't make a boneheaded move like that again." Her gaze drifted to Danny, who was still standing behind Jayne, but he had removed his hand from her shoulder. Good thing, too, because Jayne didn't trust herself not to lean back into him for support, and that wouldn't look like a person trying to stand on her own two feet. No, Jayne Murphy wasn't going to rely on her police officer brothers or Danny.

After Paige got on the elevator, Jayne turned to face Danny. "Thank you. You saved my butt."

"Happy to help."

The wind and snow were still whipping outside. "You're not going to drive home in this, are you?" she asked.

"Honestly, I haven't thought much beyond getting your dancer back here." He glanced over to the clerk. "Maybe there are some available rooms."

Jayne ran her hand across the back of her neck. "I have a few dancers camping out in my room with Hannah and my mom. Should be a fun night."

Danny tipped his head toward the casino. "Should we try our luck? I can stall until the last squall blows over."

"I think they're forecasting steady snow until morning."

"Casino never closes."

Jayne shook her head. "I'm not up for gambling tonight." She had never actually gambled. On the surface, it looked like fun, but not if her money was getting gobbled up. Jayne had never considered herself an addictive personality, but too many problems sprung from gambling gone wrong. She shook the rambling thoughts aside and glanced up at Danny. In the shadows of his handsome eyes, she thought she noticed fleeting disappointment.

"Hey, I'd be up for drink." Maybe she'd try one of those hard seltzers that were all the rage. Maybe it'd help her sleep.

"Sounds good to me." Danny placed his hand on the small of her back and led her to the bar inside the casino, stopping only briefly to show their IDs to security. Sitting on stools with their thighs inches apart, Jayne had to remind herself that she and Danny were simply friends because that's what *she* wanted them to be.

Jayne didn't think Paige was an idiot, she was simply young and trusting. And lucky. But if Jayne let Danny slip out of her grasp, she'd be the idiot.

CHAPTER TWENTY-THREE

Danny ordered their drinks and paid, leaving the change on the polished bar in the casino. A catchy song from a popular young singer who had a set of pipes on her played in the background. Jayne lifted the cranberry seltzer and took a sip, then shook her head and laughed. Man, he loved to see her laugh, something he hadn't seen lately. Heck, he hadn't seen *Jayne* much of late. Period.

"Don't you like the drink?" He looked toward the bartender, a young man with jet-black hair and big eyes. "You can order something else."

Jayne shook her head and took another sip. "It's an acquired taste." She waved off the bartender who'd interpreted their glances as needing something. He was good at his job.

"Can I help you?" the bartender asked, wiping the surface down in front of them at the same time. "Some food, maybe? Nachos? Chicken fingers."

"Yes, and yes." She laughed again. "I haven't eaten all day. Do nachos and chicken fingers sound good to you? I missed the pizza party in the lobby." She pressed a hand against her belly.

"Perfect," Danny said. The bartender promised them food in less than fifteen minutes.

"I never eat this late. It'll sit like a rock in my gut, but it'll be good going down." Jayne smiled tightly, as if imagining a future stomachache that she would surely regret.

With his elbow propped on the bar, Danny rested his cheek on his closed fist. "You okay?"

She took another sip, then set the glass down on the counter. She blinked slowly, her pretty blue eyes watching him. He wished he could see himself in her eyes, make the changes that would allow her to accept his offer of help, to protect her, without feeling like she needed to prove herself.

"It's been a day, huh?" he pressed when she didn't answer.

Jayne took a deep breath then let it out. "It's been a day."

"Any new information on Dale Diamond's death?" he asked.

Jayne eyed him skeptically. "The police want to write it off as an accidental death."

"You don't agree?"

Jayne drained her drink. The attentive bartender came over and Jayne ordered another one. He'd never seen her drink one, never mind two drinks. The bartender emptied the can into a fresh glass and slid it toward her on the bar. Danny shook his head and tipped his half-full beer bottle. He didn't usually nurse a drink, but he was stalling in hopes the storm would pass and the crews could clear the roads. Otherwise, he'd have to fork over a credit card for a room for the night. But, like gambling, it seemed like a waste of money.

"I don't think that Mr. Diamond's death was accidental," Jayne said, seeming to be holding her breath, waiting for an argument. "He was moved." She lifted a hand and pointed at Danny in exaggeration, her words growing a little sloppy, but determined. He didn't ask why she thought that because he knew she was getting to it. "The backs of his shoes were scuffed, like he was dragged and placed in the bathroom."

Danny tilted his head and studied her. "His shoes weren't scuffed before?"

Jayne shook her head, a red strand of hair falling down the center of her forehead. He resisted the urge to brush it away.

"Dale Diamond was impeccable about his appearance. Never a blob of ketchup on his shirt. A hair out of place. Or a mark on his shoes." Jayne reached over and touched a stain on Danny's shirt. "Leftover from dinner?" Her mouth twitched.

Danny brushed his sleeve, the orange stain not budging. "Not sure. I must have brushed against something." He sniffed, considering Jayne's observation about Mr. Diamond. "What did the officer have to say?"

"Told me he didn't need my two cents." Jayne rolled her eyes and shrugged. "I sensed he didn't like that I was a private investigator."

"You told him you were a PI?"

"Yeah, I thought it might hold some weight." Jayne looked up at nothing in particular, it seemed. "Maybe it was when I told him I didn't have my license yet. That I worked for Teddy Wysocki. I don't know. But he didn't listen." Jayne ran her hand across her cheek thoughtfully. "I got the sense that he *wanted* it to be an accident. Like, it was too much work to investigate something more."

Danny tilted his head, a question on his lips that he bit back. Questioning her reasoning was what had jeopardized their relationship. However, would he always have to watch what he said? Jayne was a smart woman. Why did he feel the need to question her?

Jayne leaned toward him, shoulder to shoulder. She smelled of a fruity drink and her familiar shampoo and laundry detergent—he'd figured out that scent when he did a load of laundry at her house. "Aren't you going to poke holes in my theory?" Her tone had a familiar defensiveness softened by alcohol.

She bumped his shoulder briefly, then spun on the stool to square off with him. He did the same, their knees colliding. She shifted and their knees interlocked, like a couple who had been together a long time. Danny went to shift his chair back when Jayne touched his thigh and lifted her unfocused gaze to him. "You look like a deer caught in headlights," she said, then giggled. She squeezed his thigh, apparently unaware of the effect she was having on him. Or maybe she did, and that was the whole point.

Danny reached down and covered her hand and decided to focus on the topic at hand. "Unfortunately, I don't have any jurisdiction in Niagara Falls, but I could make a few calls. See if I can get answers on why they're so quick to write it off as an accidental death."

Jayne slid her hand out from under his, then playfully punched him in his arm. He worried sober Jayne would be truly annoyed with tipsy Jayne for letting her guard down. "I know, I know," she said, like a middle schooler who was the only one who knew the answer to a challenging math problem. "The hotel has had some recent bad press regarding drug overdoses on their property. They're afraid of scaring away family-friendly events like dance competitions." Jayne took another swig of her drink. "Can you imagine the hubbub if someone like Mr. Diamond was murdered while here to emcee a dance competition? They'd lose a ton of business."

"I can ask a few questions," Danny said tentatively, unsure if she wanted him to get involved. "See what else I can uncover."

She tapped his thigh playfully again. "Teddy's doing some digging too. He always has the dirt." Jayne narrowed her gaze, then her eyes opened wide, as if she had just remembered something. "With everything going on, we didn't talk much about Carol Anne." Her gaze seemed to look right through him, like she knew he had only told her part of the story.

"What do you want to know?"

"I want to know why you didn't tell me she was in the Greens' house."

"I didn't want to worry you."

She lifted an eyebrow. "Do you think I should be worried?"

"It appears someone was sleeping in Melinda's bed. My guess would be Carol Anne." He kept his gaze on Jayne while she stared someplace on the worn floor off to their left. The celebratory sounds of a nearby slot machine rose above the din. He let himself track the sound. An older woman sat stoically at a machine, her gaze fixed on the flashing animals and squiggling lines on the screen. What was the attraction of gambling if she couldn't get excited when she won? He turned back to Jayne, who seemed to be holding back a million questions. Maybe she'd want to be sober for this discussion. Or maybe the reasons she asked him about it now was because she had a buzz.

"Are you going to make me drag it out of you?" Jayne pressed.

"There were binoculars next to the window facing your house. I saw a few other things that made me uneasy."

Jayne nodded, resting her chin on her fist. "You don't have to hide things from me. I'm a big girl." She hiccupped then winced as if something pained her. "Excuse me."

Danny smiled, wishing they were here under different circumstances, on a date, without all their shared past. The baggage.

Even though they'd likely never get a fresh start, he hoped they could find a way to carve out a future together.

CHAPTER TWENTY-FOUR

A shudder scurried down Jayne's spine. The alcohol that had initially given her a nice fuzzy feeling sloshed in her gut, making her question her choices tonight. Out of the corner of her eye, the flashing lights from the gambling machines threatened to trigger a migraine. She remembered why she rarely drank. Eventually the good feelings turned to nausea and a throbbing behind her eyes.

"How do you know it was Carol Anne in the house?" Jayne asked the question even though she knew in her gut it was her. It had to be. Who else would hunker down in Melinda's room with an eye on Jayne's house? But Danny didn't rely strictly on feelings. He preferred solid evidence to back it up.

"I'll show you when we get home tomorrow, okay? Can you trust me?" Danny sounded so darn sincere.

"Yes, I'll trust you."

Danny swirled what was left of his beer in the dark brown bottle. "I drove out to see Carol Anne early this morning at her mother's RV. She claims she was home Friday night with the snow and all."

Jayne ran her hand over the back of her neck, trying to

shake the weight of the foreboding pressing down on her lungs. "But you don't believe her."

"Carol Anne is a practiced liar. However, as of now, I have no way to prove it. The trailer park looked snowed in. Not sure how she would have traveled in and out of there."

"For argument's sake, let's say it was Carol Anne. Why would she throw a brick through the window?" She studied Danny's face. He didn't react, which meant he'd been wondering the same thing. "Does that make sense? If she was squatting in her dead stepsister's bedroom, damaging the property would only give herself away."

"Carol Anne is a troubled woman. I don't presume to know how she thinks."

Jayne nodded. "Maybe she was bored. Maybe she'd been there for a few days." A prickling sensation made the hairs on the back of her neck come to life. Hadn't she been feeling like she was under a microscope lately? She had written it off as exhaustion. She had forced herself out of her comfort zone by taking on this PI gig. She had dismissed it all. Anger replaced her unease. She needed to hone her gut feelings, not dismiss them.

Jayne pushed her empty glass away from her. The bartender approached and she asked for a Coke. "I'm going to need a clear head. Too much going on to be fuzzy about things."

"Do you have a case you're officially working on right now?" Danny asked.

She pressed her lips together and shook her head. "It's been quiet."

"Do you like being a private investigator?" Danny asked, the question seeming to come out of nowhere.

Jayne breathed in deeply, then exhaled. "Some of it. Some of it makes me feel dirty. I hated getting involved in that messy divorce case with Paige's parents. I think that's why she's acting out." She shook her head, wishing she could straighten the teen out before she found herself in real trouble.

"That's got to be tough." A shadow crossed his face. "I'm sorry about the role my father played in that case." Chief Nolan helped fabricate damning evidence against her client. Danny had apologized before, and she had accepted the apology, but it was apparent that it still haunted him.

The sins of the father and all that.

Jayne reached out and touched his forearm. He had his shirtsleeves pushed up and his skin felt hot to the touch. "You're not your dad."

Half his mouth quirked into a grin that didn't reach his eyes. Her empathetic nature had her reaching out and cupping his jaw, the whiskers from his five o'clock shadow tickling her palm. "You are a sweet man." He turned his face into her hand and she quickly pulled it away. "Sorry." *Idiot.* She had been the one to put a halt to their relationship. Frowning, she made a show of putting her hand to her forehead. "I think I had too much to drink. And this whole Carol Anne thing..."

Yeah, keep the conversation on professional matters.

"We're going to have to keep an eye on her. Conditions of her release dictate that she stay away from her father's house. If you see her, one phone call and she'll be locked up to await trial."

Jayne swallowed. "The thought is mildly comforting." Out of the corner of her eye, she noticed a man walk into the bar shaking snow from his coat. "Looks like it's still coming down out there. I'd offer you a spot on the floor in my room, but it's already at full capacity with stranded dancers." She sighed at the thought. She'd give anything for a good night's sleep. Maybe she'd wake up with new perspective. A clear head.

She'd be grateful if she simply woke up without a pounding hangover.

Danny shifted on the stool and placed his hands on the edge of the bar. "Maybe I should check into the hotel after all." He tilted his head toward the exit. "Want to take a stroll with me?"

"Sure." Jayne slid off the stool and the floor tilted underneath her. *Ugh.*

As they headed across the lobby, Danny placed a firm hand on the small of her back. She allowed herself to wonder what it'd be like if they were a true couple, not two people with a long history who went on a few dates and flirted with something more until it got too complicated. She told herself to walk ahead of him, create some distance, but she was enjoying his presence. *That's the problem, isn't it?*

Freddie was still working the front desk when Danny checked to see if there were any rooms available. The clerk didn't make eye contact with her as he had done earlier. Jayne hated that some men felt like they could gawk, but immediately fell in line when another man was present. She was almost drunk enough to call him on it, but then decided she was too tired for anymore nonsense.

Freddie spent an inordinate amount of time tapping away on the keyboard, apparently searching for an available room. As they waited for this young man to put the final footnotes on his dissertation, Jayne had an idea. She tugged on Danny's hand, pulling him out of earshot.

She lowered her voice to make sure she wouldn't be overheard. "Ask him if room 1997 is available?"

Danny's mouth twitched. "Diamond's room?"

Jayne nodded. "Do you think they've released it?" She was unable to hide the giddy hope from her voice. "We could see if the police missed anything."

"Housekeeping will have cleaned the room." Skepticism

shone in his eyes, something that might have bothered her if she wasn't convinced they'd find something. She felt it in her bones.

Danny gave her a quick nod, then spun around and returned to the counter, pulling Jayne by the hand. "My girlfriend and I were hoping to get the same room we had last time we were here. I came here to surprise her and…" He draped his arm around her shoulders and pulled her close. Jayne realized she probably should have told Danny this kid gave her access to the cameras outside Dale Diamond's room and would more than likely realize this cover story was BS. So, she decided she'd play along to see how far they could get.

Jayne squeezed Danny's hand that dangled over her shoulder and leaned playfully against his solid chest. He must have been spending the time they'd been apart ramping up his strength training. She had missed these arms. "Yes, room 1997. Is it free?" She stopped herself from batting her eyelashes, realizing that would have been a step too far.

"Let me see," Freddie said. He went back to *tap-tap-tapping* on the keyboard. "Oh." There must have been a note in the computer about *that* room. The room where poor Mr. Diamond allegedly fell and hit his head, a blow so severe that he had expired.

"Is it available? I can't imagine you have a full house with this weather," Danny said casually.

"You'd be surprised. Lot of people got stuck downtown with the snow. We're nearing capacity."

"Oh no," Jayne said, laying it on a little too thick, at least in her ears. She was a parody of the girly-girls she wasn't especially fond of. "Won't we get our room?"

Freddy pointed at her. "Weren't you here earlier asking about that room?" He raised his eyebrows unwilling to make himself look guilty for letting her look at the security cameras.

Heat flushed over her. "Yeah..." She dipped her head shyly, "My boyfriend came here to support me. He knows how much my friend's death hit me. We thought if we checked into the room where he last stayed, it would help with the grieving process." Inwardly, she shuddered. How morbid.

Freddie shrugged and turned his focus back to the computer screen. Jayne smiled brightly—go alcohol—but inside, her patience was growing thin. He looked up. "I need to make a call."

"Hold up," Danny said with the authority of a police officer that commanded compliance. The clerk froze and lifted his eyebrows in expectation. Danny removed his arm from around Jayne and reached into his back pocket for his wallet. "The room is empty and housekeeping has turned it over," he said it as statement, not a question, probably figuring the clerk would correct him if necessary. Danny pulled out a hundred-dollar bill and slid it across the counter. "We're tired. I'd appreciate it if you could check us into room 1997. There's a big tip in it for you."

Half the clerk's mouth quirked in a grin. He was making bank tonight. He slid the bill off the counter, tucking it under some papers, before saying, "ID and credit card, please."

CHAPTER TWENTY-FIVE

A bead of sweat trickled down Jayne's back. She wasn't sure if it was the close confines of the elevator or the fact that they were about to check into the room where Dale Diamond had died. *Was murdered?* The walls began to pulse and Jayne stuck her hand out and steadied herself on Danny's arm.

"You okay?" His deep voice sounded like it was coming through a tunnel.

"Freddie at the front desk probably thinks I have a screw loose, wanting to stay in the same room where I found a dead body less than twelve hours ago." Jayne swallowed down her nausea. She was afraid she might toss her cookies in this elevator, and how humiliating would that be? She focused intently on the light bouncing along the line of numbers as they made their ascent.

"He got a big tip for his troubles." He reached down and squeezed her hand.

"You overpaid."

"What?"

"He let me look at the security cameras for fifty bucks."

Danny laughed. "You could have told me that earlier. Did you find anything?"

Jayne shook her head. "Just a shadowy figure that could have been anyone."

It suddenly got really, really hot in the elevator. Jayne blinked slowly, willing the elevator to hurry up and reach their floor. Finally, the doors slid open and she lunged out, gulping in the fresh air. Thankfully, the corridor felt about ten degrees cooler.

She breathed in and out slowly, waving off Danny's offer of help. Heck, if she waited for a minute, it would pass. Meanwhile, she vowed to never, ever, *ever* drink again. After a minute, she straightened, convinced she wasn't in imitate danger of puking and smiled at Danny sheepishly.

"Are you okay?" he asked.

"Yes. I should have stopped after one drink though." She grimaced as bile tickled the back of her throat.

"Come on." Danny tilted his head toward Mr. Diamond's room. Another shudder racked her body, but this time, it wasn't because of her stupid drinking, it was because she felt like she was walking on Mr. Diamond's grave. About twenty-four hours ago, he'd traveled this same hallway—stressed and out of sorts, if her meeting with him in the casino had been any indication—but he couldn't have known that it would have been the final moments of his life.

Did anyone?

Danny slowed in front of room 1997 and waved his keycard over the contactless keypad. He turned the handle, but the door remained locked. A hint of disappointment swept through her. He waved the keycard again. This time, the lock clicked, a light blinked green, and Danny pushed open the door. She gave him points for not insisting she go first.

The room smelled like the strong antiseptic and carpet

freshener the cleaners at the studio used to combat the stench of lots of sweaty dancer feet. She glanced around, slowly taking in the room for first impressions.

"Not sure there'll be much information to glean, considering housekeeping put the room back in order," Danny said.

Jayne couldn't help but giggle. "Thanks, Captain Obvious."

He rolled his eyes and laughed, then grew serious. "What are you thinking?"

She slowly shook her head, deep in thought. "There was something... I don't know..." She looked around again. "There was a lot going on. Housekeeping let me in, then we found his body. But..." Jayne got down on her hands and knees and looked under the bed. From her neurotic habit of checking all drawers and under beds when she stayed at hotels herself, she realized the cleaning didn't always extend to deep under the beds, based on the dust bunnies and random stuff she'd found under there. She had once learned the hard way when she had to fetch her phone under the bed skirt and ended up patting a fuzzy lollipop.

"You need help down there?" Danny asked, a hint of humor in his tone.

She glared up at him. "Yeah, move out of my light." She straightened her back, her knees digging into the carpet. "Hand me my phone. It's in the outer pocket of my purse."

Danny did as she requested and she flipped on the flashlight app. She leaned over, careful not to let her face touch the carpet. Goodness knew what was on there. She directed the light under the bed. Nothing but a few fuzzies and what looked like a stray sock under the first bed. Walking on her knees, she lumbered over to the bed closest to the door and peered underneath. At first glance, it looked pretty much the same, minus a lumpy sock. Twisting her lips, she searched again, this time more slowly when something red caught her eye. Not blood. No, something hard.

"Give me a tissue," Jayne said, keeping the light aimed at the small item, as if it might skitter off when she wasn't looking.

Danny handed her the tissue, and she reached under and picked up something red, hard, and oval shaped. Still on her knees, she leaned her hip on the edge of the bed for balance and held out her palm. "What does that look like to you?" She carefully turned it over in her palm without touching it with her bare hand. She tipped her head and, without looking at him or waiting for him to answer, she said, "A fake nail. An acrylic. Right?"

"Could be," Danny said, noncommittally. "But it could have been there for months. You've said yourself that it looks like no one has vacuumed under the beds in a while."

Jayne closed her fingers over the possible evidence and pushed to her feet. Danny grabbed her elbow to steady her. "Should we call the police?" she asked.

He studied her for a beat. "And tell them what exactly?"

"I don't know." Jayne glanced around. "We need to search every inch of this room." Danny helped her check all the drawers, the closet, the fridge, behind the dresser, and under the beds again.

Jayne sighed and plopped down on the bed and lay back, then quickly sat up, realizing the back of her hands and head were touching the hotel bedspread, something else that probably hadn't been washed in a while. "Whoa." The quick movement and the remnants of her buzz made her head spin. After her vision settled, she carefully wrapped the nail in the tissue and tucked it into the outside pocket of her purse. "I should wait until morning before making any phone calls. I'm not thinking clearly." She stood, then tilted her head back and groaned. "My room is jam-packed with dancers having a slumber party and I only want a good night's sleep."

Danny lifted his chin. "Perfectly good bed right there. You're welcome to crash in this room."

"Would that be weird?" Jayne asked, but oh, the idea of her own bed sounded heavenly.

"Weird because you'd be sharing a room with me?" A slow smile curved his full lips. "I promise to be a good boy and stay on my side of the room."

Jayne blinked slowly with heavy lids. "No, not because of you, goofball." If she hadn't been watching him, she might have missed him wince, and she immediately felt bad about it. However, once she started down a path, she kept going. "It'd be weird because a man may have been murdered in this room." She enunciated each word.

"By a woman missing a red nail," he quipped.

A woman missing a red nail? The thought whispered across her brain, then burrowed deep. Had Mr. Diamond had a visit from a girlfriend? Did he have a habit of picking up women in different cities? Had the dark shadowy form been a woman? Had he run into trouble with a prostitute? Maybe gotten robbed? *Ugh, what a way to go.* How would his family take it? At least he was a widower and wasn't potentially cheating on a wife.

"Jayne?"

She looked up, and based on the expression on his face, he must have called her name more than once. She blinked. "Sorry." She had a knack for obsessing over every possible scenario.

"You're welcome to stay here," Danny offered again.

"Thanks." Jayne washed her face and got ready for bed. When she came out of the bathroom, she glanced down at her jeans and sweater, not exactly cozy sleeping clothes.

"Here." Danny took off his soft cotton T-shirt, revealing a

white undershirt. *Darn this cold weather.* He tossed his shirt and she snatched it out of the air. "Good hand-eye coordination."

Jayne laughed awkwardly. Danny brushed past her, smelling of whatever masculine deodorant he wore and aloe, perhaps from his aftershave. "I'm going to get ready for bed." He went inside the bathroom and closed the door. She texted Hannah, who insisted all the kids were asleep and to please sleep there if it meant getting a good night's rest. Hannah followed it with a winking face emoji. Jayne ignored it.

Convinced she'd stay, Jayne changed out of her street clothes, into Danny's t-shirt, and climbed into bed. She snuggled into the plump pillow and sighed, too tired to wash her face. This was so much better than trying to find a surface to sleep on in her own hotel room.

Jayne started to doze off and maybe she had fallen asleep when she thought she heard Danny whisper, "Night, Baby Jayne." Her brother's nickname for her, and now her brother's best friend had picked it up—a private joke because she loved old Bette Davis movies. An intimacy she and Danny once shared.

Without opening her eyes, she muttered, "Night. I hope you don't snore, Danny Boy."

CHAPTER TWENTY-SIX

Danny rolled over and checked his smartwatch. It was early—very early—and the light from the moon cast across his roommate's face. Gosh, Jayne was so darn pretty, but she didn't seem to know it. And she was smarter than anyone he knew. He plumped his pillow and adjusted it under his head and kept studying her. Yet, she lacked self-confidence, which made her lash out at anyone who she thought was undermining her. Like her brother. Like him.

Their relationship had been doomed long before her big brother, Patrick, had asked Danny if he could come over after school to play when they were in elementary school. And his little sister, Jayne, with her long, curly red hair had a been a pain in his side ever since.

Lost in thought, he hadn't realized Jayne had woken up.

"Did I drool or something?" Jayne's voice cracked. He had always anticipated their first morning waking up together to be much different. Less platonic. More romantic.

Danny laughed. Jayne's hand came up to her forehead and turned her face slightly, squinting against the moonlight. "Holy moly, that's bright. What time is it?"

"Not even six."

Jayne scrunched up her cute nose and shifted, giving him the opportunity to study her profile. She drew in a deep breath and let it out. "Too early."

"I'm used to getting up at this time. My body doesn't know how to sleep in."

"Lucky for me." She cut him a sideways glance and smirked, then went back to studying the ceiling. "Danny?" She pushed to a seated position, adjusting the pillows behind her against the headboard. She crossed her arms over her chest, one bare shoulder poking out from the collar of the oversized T-shirt. "I can't stop thinking about Carol Anne."

Danny sat up and swung his legs around, sitting on the edge of the bed with the sheet concealing his boxer shorts. He braced his elbows on his thighs and scrubbed his hands over his head. "We'll keep an eye on her."

Jayne momentarily bowed her head. "I know I mentioned it before, but it still bothers me. If Carol Anne was squatting in her dad's house, why would she have thrown a rock through the window? Drawn attention to herself? What did she have to gain?"

Danny rubbed his hand across his itchy jaw. It would be driving him crazy all day until he got home and could shave it. "It doesn't make sense. You're right. Unless she was aiming for this."

"To get under my skin?" Jayne asked.

"Perhaps. She does have her share of enemies too. Her stepsister was well loved. Maybe someone realized she was staying there and wanted her to be found out. Or maybe it was coincidental. Someone completely random, looking to vandalize an empty house, knowing its history. People can be evil."

"What about Kyle? Remember that creepy photo he took of Melinda from the same window? Maybe he came back for old times' sake," Danny said, thinking out loud, but it didn't ring true. "Part of the condition of her release was that she stays away from her stepmother and father's house. Why risk it?"

"You know Carol Anne was in my grade?" Jayne said.

Danny was a year older, but he didn't have much of a recollection of her. People tended to hang out with kids in their year, that was it.

"We hung out when we were little," she continued, "you know, when you were happy to have a friend regardless of whether you had anything in common. We grew apart when it was obvious that we weren't much alike." Jayne drew in a deep breath and released it. "She resented me for being close to her stepsister, Melinda. The accident that killed her happened in a rage of jealousy. Do you think..." she sniffed and rubbed her chilly arms, "...she's fixated on me now?"

Danny sat up straight. He resisted the urge to move over to her bed and pull her into a comforting embrace, but he didn't want to jeopardize their tenuous truce. He didn't want her to accuse him of being overly protective. But wasn't she looking for reassurance?

Reassurance he couldn't give her, especially not while sitting in his boxer shorts.

"She's unstable," Danny said.

Jayne straightened her legs under the blankets and dragged her fingers through her red, curly hair, mussed from a restless night of sleep. "Great, one more thing I have to figure out. At least we got Paige safely back, now we have to figure out if someone hurt Dale Diamond and if Carol Anne is stalking me. One out of three..." Her tone sounded droll.

Danny let a beat a silence stretch between them, and then decided now or never. "You can count on me. I'll help you in any way I can."

Jayne dropped her hands and laughed, an awkward sound.

"Maybe a few extra patrols around my house until after Carol Anne's trial?"

Danny smacked his thighs and smiled. "Done." He gathered the sheet around his waist and headed toward the bathroom. "I'm going to jump into the shower. Maybe we can grab breakfast before the hotel restaurant gets crowded."

CHAPTER TWENTY-SEVEN

Jayne tipped the mug and drained the last bit of coffee. She was starting to feel human. The waitress must have been watching their table because she appeared, offering a refill the second Jayne set the mug down. She made a cutting gesture above her mug with her hand. "No, thank you."

Danny nodded and the young woman topped him off instead. She pulled out a slip from a pocket on her hip. "Here's the check. No hurry."

"Looks like we got here just in time," Jayne said. Several groups of young dancers with exasperated, exhausted-looking chaperones—most often a dance mom—waited with them for an available table. Miss Gigi, from the competing studio across town, was dining with a few mothers. Jayne had been so busy all weekend, she hadn't seen Gigi since check-in.

Jayne had called Hannah with an offer to help get her mother and the girls ready for the day, but Hannah had said her mother was already dressed and helping wrangle the dancers. *This is truly Mom's environment.*

"Maybe we should give up our table," Danny suggested.

"Sure." Jayne placed her hand over the check and dragged it toward her. "After I pay this, I'm going to order a bunch of breakfast sandwiches for the dancers who stayed overnight in my room. I told Hannah to text me when they're headed down. This way, they won't have to wait to eat."

Danny tilted his head and a protest seemed to die on his lips. "Thank you. I'll leave the tip."

"Thanks." Jayne slid her credit card out of her wallet and placed it on top of the bill.

After they paid, they headed toward the host stand to place their to-go order when she spotted Hannah, Miss Natalie, and three dancers seated at a large, round table. Jayne locked gazes with Danny for a heartbeat. "Time for second breakfast," they said in unison. Things could be so easy with him.

"Hey, I thought you were going to text me," Jayne said. "I was about to order you guys breakfast-to-go."

"We got ready in record time," Hannah said. "So, we rushed down here. Join us."

Jayne kissed her mother on the cheek and the woman smiled politely, as if she had been greeted by a stranger. The warm feelings from spending the morning with Danny had chilled a fraction with reality suddenly crashing over her.

Seated around the table, the girls chatted about their adventures over the past twenty-four hours. Lily, the youngest said, "Are we going home today or are we stuck here?" The question held no amount of concern, but rather excitement about the possibilities of having another sleepover at the hotel and missing a day of school. All the adults, including Miss Natalie, looked less enthusiastic, instead fantasizing about sleeping in their own beds in their own houses. Thankfully, the roads had been mostly cleared and all the dancers had rides home, including the girls whose moms had been stranded at a nearby restaurant yesterday. They had grabbed a room at a different hotel and were due to arrive here soon.

Lily sat next to Jayne, glancing at her phone, then up at a nearby table. Jayne hadn't realized Amber Mack was in the restaurant nursing a cup of coffee across from JR. "That lady is the one who gave me the 'biggest smile' award."

Jayne leaned in close. "You do have the biggest smile."

"Do you think she'd give me her autograph?" Lily seemed absolutely starstruck by the Amber. Maybe this was one aspect of the job that had kept Dale Diamond doing this gig well into his sixties—that and the fact he was supporting his daughter, an aspiring dancer in New York City.

Jayne pushed away from the table and stood. She held out her hand, indicating the little dancer join her. Jayne leaned down and whispered. "Go up, say, 'excuse me, may I have your autograph?'" She suspected no one could resist a cute little girl. Lily froze in her tracks and no amount of nudging would get her to move. Finally, Jayne said, "Come on. I'll ask for you."

Lily nodded excitedly. Jayne took her hand and they approached the table. Amber lowered her coffee mug and shot Jayne a pained expression. "Excuse me," Jayne said before she lost her nerve.

"Yes?" There was an annoyed edge to Amber's tone.

"Sorry to bother you," Jayne said, reaching back to gently guide the dancer closer to the table. "Lily would love your autograph."

The woman tilted her head, then a smile parted her lips. "Of course."

Lily handed the woman a ballpoint pen with the hotel logo on it and a piece of paper that Jayne had found on the bottom of her purse. The woman seemed to hesitate a minute before taking the pen. Jayne's heart stopped. The woman had perfectly manicured red fingernails.

Jayne's pulse rose in her cheeks. "Thank you," her voice squeaked. "The dancers really look up to you."

Stop babbling. Focus.

"Amber Mack is going to be the next representative of Superstar Dance Power, the face of the next generation of dancers," JR said.

The woman smoothed a hand across her hair and pressed her red lips together, preening for an audience of one. She might ooze composure and charm, but she was cold, cold, cold.

Jayne watched the woman sign her name with a flourish. When she handed the autograph to Lily, Jayne noticed a missing red nail.

Danny made small talk with Miss Natalie while Jayne took one of her students across the restaurant to visit with a couple of the organizers of the dance competition. Laughter rose from the table across the room, awkward and high-pitched, drawing his attention. When Jayne turned around, she looked like she had seen a ghost. He furrowed his brow, trying to imagine what was going on behind those stricken eyes.

Jayne returned and helped the little girl into her chair, then whispered into Danny's ear. "It was her. Amber Mack. She's missing a red nail."

Danny resisted looking toward the table of the woman who had given the little girl her autograph.

"What is it?" Hannah asked, clearly frustrated that she was sitting all the way across the table and couldn't make out their whispers.

"Nothing, nothing," Danny repeated, then stood and took

Jayne's hand and led her to the exit. "What's going on?" He glanced around to make sure no one could overhear her.

"Amber Mack is missing a red nail. And now that Dale is dead, she's taking over as the master of ceremonies for the organization. Dale's job." Jayne opened her eyes wide, telegraphing that A+B equals C. *Obviously!* "What better motivation? We have to call Chief Ross. They need to take her into custody. Question her." Jayne was vibrating with excitement at having apparently solved the mystery.

Danny gave it a moment's thought. They had to do this by the book. "Let me give him a call."

While he was making calls, Jayne paced back and forth. Before he finished, she placed her hand on his bicep and whispered, "They're leaving. We need to stop them."

"Um, they're leaving," Danny said into the phone.

"You're basing this off a chipped nail?" the chief said over the phone.

Danny turned his back to the crowded restaurant. "We need to sort this out. How long before you can be here?"

Chief Ross sighed. "Twenty minutes."

Danny ended the call and turned to Jayne. "The chief will be here in twenty minutes."

Jayne rolled her eyes and strode over to a departing Amber and her boss.

"Wait! Jayne!" Danny called. *What is she doing?*

CHAPTER TWENTY-EIGHT

Jayne's pulse roared in her ears. She'd done far more stressful things than run her mouth for twenty minutes to prevent someone from getting away. Many people could probably vouch that she had successfully prevented someone from going about their day when she wasn't even trying.

"Miss Mack," Jayne called out, ignoring Danny and drawing the woman's attention, "thank you so much for taking the time to give my dancer your autograph. These young dancers really look up to performers." Jayne was flying by the seat of her pants.

The petite woman smiled tightly, clearly annoyed at being detained again. JR patted her hand. "Our Uber should be here."

A knot twisted in Jayne's gut. "They'll text you when they're here. Don't go outside. It's too cold." Jayne gave an exaggerated shudder. "Are you headed to the airport? Have you made sure your flight hasn't been canceled or delayed?"

JR gave her a curious gaze, as if to say, "Why do you care?" He seemed to be one of those people who only paid attention when something was of interest to him. "As a matter of fact, our flights are delayed," JR said in the slow, unaffected way he had, like any conversation was below him. "We're moving to a hotel overlooking the falls, since we're stuck here anyway."

"Oh, I hadn't realized you were a couple." *Stop talking, stop talking, stop talking. Didn't JR have on a wedding ring?* Open mouth insert foot. But she had to do what she had to do to hold them here until the NFPD arrived. "You'll be working together twenty-four seven now that you have Mr. Diamond's job." Oh, goodness, her face heated from the cringe-worthiness of her forced dialogue.

Amber's lips twitched as she casually swiped her finger across the screen of her cell phone, perhaps double-checking the location of the Uber driver. As if she had taken the necessary time to craft an appropriate response, she sighed. "I would never in a million years have wanted this job under these circumstances. Poor Mr. Diamond. He loved being the face of Superstar Dance Power."

JR cleared his throat. His eyes shooting daggers. "For what it matters, we are *not* a couple. Just coworkers." Of course, that's the part of the conversation he'd focus on.

If Jayne hadn't been studying Amber's face, she might have missed the subtle peevish expression that tightened her lips, then disappeared. It was a slight variation of the aggrieved look when Jayne had insinuated there had been some cheer on Amber's part when she learned she would benefit from Dale Diamond's untimely death.

JR casually brushed the back of his hand against her arm as if cautioning her to be quiet. *What's that all about?* Jayne glanced over at Danny to see if he'd noticed, but his focus was trained on the exit, perhaps looking for a patrol car.

"Oh, I didn't mean to offend you," Jayne said, growing braver now that Danny was standing behind her. "Have you met my friend, Danny Nolan?"

Amber's big eyes moved to Danny, then back to Jayne. "I don't think we have. Nice to meet you." Her expression was stoic and she didn't offer her hand.

JR nodded, apparently too self-important to be bothered to utter a greeting.

"Um..." *Now or never, Jayne.* "I ran into Mr. Diamond in the casino on Friday night. He seemed distressed." Not to mention drunk and chatty. *Had* the alcohol played a part in his death?

Amber stopped fidgeting with her phone and looked up and blinked, her long, dark lashes sweeping against her flawless skin. Her brown eyebrows were lost behind her platinum blonde bangs.

JR spoke first. "I've never been much a fan of gambling. Seems a waste of money."

"Perhaps," Jayne said, "Mr. Diamond was worried he was going to be replaced."

Jayne let the silence stretch between them, watching their reaction. Finally, JR said, "I suppose that's water under the bridge."

"Because he's dead?" Danny asked, his deep voice washing over her.

JR lifted a perfectly manicured eyebrow. A subtle gesture. Was this some sort of tell? "Tragic," he said, simply.

Jayne cleared her throat. "It is."

JR looked like he was about to say something when he suddenly lifted his cell phone. "Our ride's here."

Amber adjusted the strap of her designer purse over her shoulder and grabbed the handle of her rolling suitcase. "Safe travels."

Jayne's mind went blank. "We have to stop them!" she said in a hushed tone. "Danny..." She tugged on his arm, but he didn't budge.

"We have no authority to detain them."

His calm was beyond frustrating. "Danny!" Despite her rising panic, she was able to keep her voice down.

He turned and met her gaze. "We know where they're going. They don't know what we found. They have no reason to flee. The police department will find them and talk this through."

She tilted her head and studied him. "So you don't think I'm grasping at straws?"

"I never said that. You may have uncovered a key piece of evidence in this case."

The warmth of his approval rained down over her. *Darn, why am I so needy?* "Thanks."

Jayne glanced out the windows overlooking the street. "If they get away, I'm going to..." She dropped her shoulders. She had to trust the process. But *she* would love to be able to make the big arrest.

Just once.

CHAPTER TWENTY-NINE

Jayne got her mother settled in her favorite chair in the family room, then brought the overnight bags in from the trunk. Thankfully, by late afternoon, the snow had let up, giving the plows time to clear the roads. They had to leave Niagara Falls with the confidence the police would follow up with Amber and JR. Had the woman killed Mr. Diamond? She was petite, but if he *had* been inebriated... Maybe they'd argued. Maybe it had been an accident. Jayne had a hard time turning her brain off.

In the kitchen, she filled the kettle. Across the dark, snow-covered yard sat the Greens' house. A gutter hung loose at the back and she could imagine, but couldn't quite see, the plywood covering Melinda's bedroom window. A light snapped on in the house next to the Greens'. Hannah must be in her bedroom unpacking from the weekend. Gosh, that girl was a Godsend. Jayne would have never been able to manage without Hannah.

By the time Jayne had made her mother a hot cup of black tea, Miss Natalie was already dozing. Jayne settled on the couch and tipped her head back, closing her eyes.

Ah, home...

A quiet knock sounded on the door and Jayne sat up and blinked. She must have dozed off. She shook her head, trying to shake the confusion. Then everything that had happened over the past few days came flooding back.

Mr. Diamond's death.

Paige's disappearance and return.

Carol Anne being released...potentially stalking her.

The knock came again. She glanced over at her mom, whose head was tilted at an awkward angle. As soon as Jayne took care of whoever was the door, she'd have to help her mom get to bed. Jayne rubbed the back of her aching neck out of empathy as she walked toward the front door. She sighed heavily, wondering if her brother was already bringing the dog back. Like he couldn't mind her till morning? Jayne loved Trinket; she just wanted a solid night's sleep. She went to the side door and was surprised to find a sheepish Hannah standing there. Jayne pushed the door open. "Come on in." Reading something on her face, Jayne added, "Is something wrong?"

"Um...no, not really." The young woman kicked off her boots and slid off her coat, revealing flannel PJs. She shrugged shyly. "My parents extended their trip. I'm a little freaked staying home alone after everything that happened" —she gestured with her chin in the general direction of the Greens' house — "over there the other night."

"That's understandable. You can sleep in the guest room." Jayne was happy for the teen's company.

"The couch is fine," Hannah said, her shoulders relaxing away from her ears.

"No, I have a perfectly good guest room." Jayne put the tea kettle back on. "Tea or hot chocolate?"

"Do you have marshmallows?"

"Yep." Jayne laughed. "Hot chocolate, then?"

After getting her mother to bed, Jayne made them warm drinks and they settled on the couch. Jayne aimed the remote at the TV when some game show came on. "There's got to be something better than this on." She shifted on the couch, bending her knee under her to face Hannah. Did we finish that series about the guy who was taking advantage of women he met on that dating app, then cut them into little pieces?"

Hannah giggled nervously. "I'm never going to find a boyfriend."

"Not like that, you won't." Jayne clicked through a few stations and stopped on a series where the narrator was recounting a woman's last moments in her apartment in Chicago. "Have you seen this one?"

Hannah scratched her forehead.

After Melinda died, Jayne had never expected to share her interest in true crime shows with someone else. Her mother tolerated them—sometimes—but mostly she preferred the likes of *Wheel of Fortune* and sitcoms.

"I did see this one. The guy got in through an open window off the fire escape." Hannah shook her head in disbelief. "You know, I think we binged several series with a dating app gone wrong premise." Hannah pointed her finger, growing more animated. "Oh, is that the one with the actress who was in that other show we liked?"

It was Jayne's turn to laugh. She flicked over to one of the popular streaming services and found the series they had been halfway through. "It feels so much later than..." She turned and squinted at the tiny blue numbers on the microwave clock across the open floor plan. "It's only eight."

"I can't wait until the evenings are lighter longer," Hannah said.

"Me too."

They both got quiet when the episode started. Almost

simultaneously, they looked at each other. "Didn't we see this episode?"

Jayne paused the show. "We're quite the pair." She clicked through to the next episode when a quiet rap sounded on the front door.

Hannah grabbed Jayne's knee. "What if it's *her*?"

There was no mistaking who *her* was. Jayne squeezed Hannah's hand and set it aside. "I'm sorry I introduced you to true crime shows."

"Shows? We've been living inside our *own* crime drama this past weekend." Hannah waggled her eyebrows playfully, but in the depths of her eyes, Jayne detected real concern.

Jayne stood. "I promise I'll peek out the window before I open the door."

She found herself walking tentatively to the front door, her frayed nerves ready to snap. Her empathetic nature made her susceptible to every shift in mood around her, including Hannah's apprehension. The poor teen was too afraid to sleep alone in her own house because of what Jayne had exposed her to.

Jayne peered out one of the sidelights and found Danny, facing the street, his breath rising in a puff above his head. "It's just Danny," she called, to reassure her guest. She tugged open the door, holding her flannel closed around her neck against the frigid January air.

He slowly turned around, his boot tamping down the snow on her uncleared porch. His mouth curved into a sly smile. "Just Danny, huh?"

Jayne laughed. "Sorry about that. All things considered, it could have been anyone at the door."

"Yet you answered it."

"Not before making sure you weren't a serial killer." Jayne tipped her head toward the side window, then grew somber.

"You have news?" She figured the Niagara Falls police would reach out to a fellow officer before they contacted her.

Danny opened his mouth, then glanced over his shoulder. That's when Jayne realized how rude she was being. "Come on in. It's cold out there."

He stepped into the foyer and narrowed his gaze. "Where's Trinket?" The little white fluff ball was usually the first person to enthusiastically greet Danny at the door.

"My brother's dog sitting."

Danny nodded.

"Join us. Hannah and I are having hot chocolate."

"No, I'll give you a quick update and be on my way. It's been a long weekend."

"Yeah, what's going on?" Jayne hooked her arm over the newel on the foot of the stairway.

"Chief Ross called me. They caught up with Miss Mack and Juan Ramos at their hotel. Miss Mack insists she wasn't ever in Dale's room. Juan vouched for her."

"JR."

Danny tilted his head in confusion.

"JR. Juan Ramos goes by JR."

"JR is her alibi."

Jayne ran a hand through her hair. "What about the red acrylic fingernail?"

"Until they get forensics, they don't have any proof." Danny crossed his arms over his broad chest. He smelled of cold air and something familiar Jayne wasn't willing to explore right now. Thank goodness Hannah was in the other room, a chaperone of sorts.

"And housekeeping already cleaned the room." They had witnessed that firsthand. The room had been generally cleaned, leaving only the dust bunnies—and the fingernail—under the bed. "Did Chief Ross mention why the hotel had been so quick to release the room? And why the police never looked at the security video?"

"Chief Ross told me to stick to crimes in Tranquility when I asked one too many questions. So, I called Office Fiorella. He told me he was working on the orders of his boss," Danny said, then sniffed. The tip of his nose was red from the cold. "Chief Ross wanted this case closed. Apparently, he was under a lot of pressure due to crime in and around the casino and hotel. Political pressure. No need to make Mr. Diamond's death into something it wasn't."

Jayne furrowed her brow and Danny continued, "The hotel, casino, and convention center are the lifeblood of the community. If people start perceiving it as dangerous, say goodbye to dance competitions, craft shows, professional conventions. *Poof*. They all go away."

Jayne sighed heavily and lowered herself onto the bottom step. "What a mess."

"The chief serves at the pleasure of the mayor. At least, that's how it is in Tranquility." Danny laughed a mirthless sound. "That's how my father found himself out of a job as chief. He got caught up in the politics and made some unethical decisions."

"What am I going to tell Dale's daughter?" Jayne looked up to find Danny watching her closely. "Oh well, too bad about your dad," she said, answering her own question in a way she really didn't want to.

Deeper in the house, the phone rang. She would have let it go to voicemail, but she had set a special ringtone unique for Teddy. She pulled herself up from the stairs and brushed past Danny. "That's my boss. Maybe he has something. He's a master at digging up information," she called back to him as she rushed to the kitchen. She dug her phone out of her purse, fearing he'd hang up before she found it. Teddy was so twitchy about phones, even if she called him right back, there was no guarantee that he'd answer. He hated telemarketers and refused to get caller ID.

"Teddy," she said, expecting the heavy black handset to be halfway to the cradle.

"I was able to track down a few of the dance instructors from Superstar Dance Dance or whatever it's called."

Impressed, Jayne pulled out a chair at the kitchen table and dropped into it. "Superstar Dance Power." She propped her elbows on the table and held the phone to her ear. "How did you manage that?"

"I'm a PI." Teddy laughed, a wet sound that rumbled up from deep in his throat.

"Tell me," Jayne said. She gestured at the kitchen chair across from hers for Danny.

"I talked to two different dance instructors. Apparently, Juan Ramos is having an affair with Amber Mack."

Jayne rubbed her hand across her forehead, her heart rate beginning to race. "They did look chummy, but they claimed they were just business associates." *Of course they did.* "Okay, I can buy that. Thanks for letting me know."

Teddy made a noise that sounded a lot like, "Do you think that's all I have?"

"Are you going to make me drag it out of you?" Jayne asked, shaking her head and rolling her eyes in Danny's general direction.

"Cases have been few and far between, give me this small amount of pleasure in telling you what I've uncovered," Teddy said.

She clicked on the speaker icon on her cell phone screen so Danny could hear both sides of the conversation. "By the way, you're on speaker. Danny's here."

"Yup," Teddy said by way of acknowledgment. "Turns out Miss Mack was getting impatient to become the face of Super Super Duper Star Dance competition."

Jayne laughed quietly. "Superstar Dance Power."

"Whatever. Miss Mack threatened to tell JR's wife about their affair if he didn't give her a promotion, but Mr. Diamond—"

"Had three years left on his contract."

"Ah, I'm training you well, grasshopper." A laugh-cough sounded over the line. Jayne imagined Teddy lighting his cigarette at that exact moment.

Jayne looked across the table and locked eyes with Danny. She lifted an eyebrow. "Based on what you're telling me, JR had more motivation to kill Dale Diamond than Amber had. Make his girlfriend happy and eliminate the risk of his wife finding out about his infidelity, however extreme. But what about the red nail under the bed?"

"We don't know that it was hers," Teddy said.

"The woman was missing a red nail." Too coincidental. Jayne rested her cheek on her fist, her elbow planted on the table. "It doesn't look good." She cleared her throat. "Tell me, how did you track down the dance instructors?"

"Social media."

Jayne jerked her head back. "Ah, I see the master is also learning from the grasshopper." She angled her head, looking in Danny's direction, but not really seeing him. "How exactly did you track them on social media? You don't have a cell phone."

"I have a computer." Teddy laughed, clearly amused by her. "But maybe I should get one of those newfangled thingies."

She doubted the curmudgeon would get a smartphone, but he obviously still had tricks up his sleeve.

"What's next?" Jayne asked.

"I'm not done." Teddy spoke in the excited tone that reminded her of the TV ads exclaiming, "But wait...there's more!" So Jayne waited. "I did some digging on that dance company. Turns out they're in serious financial trouble."

"So JR couldn't afford an expensive divorce."

"*Or* an expensive master of ceremonies. Dale Diamond's contract was very lucrative. I imagine JR would be able to hire a new, young person for a fraction of the cost."

"Thanks, Teddy, good info."

"Yeah, yeah, I'll keep digging. Talk soon."

Jayne ended the call and tossed the phone down on the table. It hit with a solid *thwack*, and she winced. She picked it up and double-checked the screen. Phew. All good. "That would have sucked if I cracked it." She looked up and met Danny's gaze. "What do you make of that?"

"Same as you. Another person has motive. It doesn't rule Amber out, though." Danny ran his hand across his mouth. "I'll reach out to Chief Ross in Niagara Falls. Let him know what Teddy found."

"Do you think he'll follow up on it? Like you said, they're eager to make his death look accidental. They're worried about the crime rates."

"And he's likely to tell me to stick to crime in Tranquility, but we can't ignore this. Besides, a targeted murder would be better than random crime. That's what spooks people away."

"This case isn't over. JR or Amber had something to do with it. We must find justice for Mr. Diamond. For his daughter." Jayne's shoulders sagged. "I'm never going to be an effective investigator without the weight of the police behind me." Her frustration was growing.

"If it wasn't for you, the case would already be closed." Hannah wrapped her hands around the back of an empty kitchen chair. She pointed toward the TV with her thumb, indicating that she hadn't been sitting that far away. "Sorry, couldn't help but overhear."

"My own personal cheer squad," Jayne said.

"It's true," Hannah said.

"How are you doing, Hannah?" Danny asked.

"Good. No complaints. Any word on Carol Anne?" Hannah asked, and Jayne found herself holding her breath. With everything else, she hadn't thought about the unstable woman for a few minutes.

"Nothing since I stopped by the trailer park Saturday morning."

"Hey," Jayne said, "you wanted me to check out Melinda's room. To see what was out of place."

"It's cold and snowy. Are you sure you want to do that now?" Danny asked.

"It won't take long. I have keys. I know the Greens won't mind. They'll want to know what's going on," Jayne said. "After talking to Teddy, I'm supercharged. I won't be able to relax anyway."

"Okay, sure," Danny said.

"Hannah, do you mind if we run over there while you stay with Miss Natalie?"

"Not at all, but you're going to miss the best part of this episode." Hannah's tone was jocular with a hint of sarcasm.

"Who needs true crime TV when you're living it?" Jayne asked, unable to stop herself from giggling. She was truly losing it. "I'll lock the door behind us when we head out."

"Trust me, I'll be deadlocking it right behind you," Hannah said.

CHAPTER THIRTY

Jayne handed Danny the key and he unlocked the Greens' house. They'd had to traipse through a foot of snow in the adjoining backyards to get here. The one perk of all the snow was that it indicated no one else had been lurking nearby—recently, anyway.

Danny pushed the door open and held out his hand, allowing Jayne to go ahead of him. The closed-up smell was the first thing that hit her. She held the collar of her coat to her nose. "That's ripe." She pressed the foot pedal on the garbage can and looked inside. It was empty. "I wonder where it's coming from." She felt like she was avoiding the inevitable. She hadn't been back in Melinda's bedroom since shortly after she died, which wasn't that long ago, and her emotions hovered just below the surface.

Apparently sensing her concern, Danny gently touched the small of her back. "I'm sorry. I should have been more sensitive. You don't have to go in there. I can talk you through it."

She shook her head slowly. "No, this is important." If Danny thought she needed to see something in person, she'd have to put her big-girl pants on. Without further delay, she strolled down the hallway, the same one she used to go down when she checked on Melinda when she babysat her as a young girl. Melinda hadn't been much younger than Jayne, but Mrs. Green had hired her to keep her daughter company when she went out. Tears threatened, but she held them back. In her short life, Jayne had learned how quickly life could change. In a split second.

A heart attack.

A gunshot.

A swerve.

A chance encounter.

Jayne cleared her throat and drew in a deep breath. "What are you thinking?" she asked, stopping in front of Melinda's closed bedroom door.

"When you open the door, take the room in. Tell me what you see. Anything unusual. Out of place."

Jayne nodded. Danny honestly seemed to value her investigative skills. An inexplicable wave of apprehension washed over her. She reached down and turned the handle, pushing the door open. Nostalgia and grief sucker punched her in the solar plexus. "Oh man, I miss Melinda. She should be making plans for her move to New York City right now. Complaining how expensive rent is going to be. Lining up auditions."

Danny cupped her elbow and whispered in her ear. "Don't do this to yourself. Tell me, what do you see?" Anything that would prove Carol Anne had been squatting in her dead sister's bedroom.

Melinda's bed was unmade. There was a pair of binoculars by the window. Jayne looked up at Danny. "Was Carol Anne watching my house?" He didn't answer, so Jayne walked deeper into the bedroom. A pair of sunglasses caught her attention on the bedside table. Jayne picked them up and turned them over in her hands. "These are mine." She locked gazes with Danny. "I thought I lost them, or that the dog got them."

"Where did you last see them?"

"I usually put them in my purse and I keep my purse on the back of the chair in the kitchen." Realization sent a new flush of pinpricks racing across her flesh. "Carol Anne was in my house."

"*If* this was Carol Anne," Danny reminded her.

"If it was Carol Anne," Jayne repeated. "Who else would it be?"

Jayne slid the glasses into her coat pocket. She loved these glasses. She turned around, slowing to take in every inch of this room that had been so familiar to her. Nothing else seemed too far out of the ordinary, other than signs of recent activity, like a glass of water on the desk and a crumbled-up sweatshirt on the floor. "Someone was in here, and my gut tells me it was Melinda's stepsister. What does she want?"

Jayne sighed deeply, then answered her own question. "She's fixated on me. She was jealous of Melinda because her father lavished all his attention on his stepdaughter. Then, after she died, Mr. Green gave the dance studio a huge donation. So even with Melinda gone, his own daughter was still a second-class citizen." Jayne pulled the comforter up on the bed and sat down on its edge, staring out over the darkened yard at her own house. She had to tilt her head a bit to see around the plywood covering the broken pane of glass. Through the open blinds at her house, Jayne could see her mother's favorite chair. Hannah was sitting on the couch with her legs crossed, working on her knitting. Jayne turned her head and looked at Danny. "She sat right here and watched everything we did. Remind me to close the blinds." She wasn't sure why she had left them open in the first place. Probably out of laziness.

No more.

"What doesn't make sense to me is why she'd break the window, especially from the outside? If she had gotten away with living here, why make her presence known?" They had discussed this before with no answers.

"Maybe Carol Anne was staying here and someone else broke the window?"

Jayne bit her bottom lip, considering. "Someone who's as unstable as she is. She probably met some people where she was being held." Jayne sighed again. "Just great. Carol Anne is a people pleaser. The last thing we need is for her to be under the influence of someone who also lacks sound judgment. Maybe we can reach out to the facility where she was staying? See if she had any friends?"

Danny placed his hand on her shoulder. "It's a solid theory. I can make some phone calls tomorrow if you'd like."

Jayne nodded, realizing she was foolish for pushing him away. "I'd appreciate that." She reached into her pocket and felt her sunglasses. "You know, I might leave my blinds open, but I never leave the house unlocked."

"I talked to Finn about getting fingerprints in this bedroom, but he said if it *was* Carol Anne, it wouldn't matter. This was her home too. It would be reasonable to find her prints here. It wouldn't mean that she had forced her way in recently."

"What about on the sunglasses?" Jayne regretted fingering them up.

"I checked. No prints."

"Carol Anne is unstable, but apparently, she's no dummy. How are we going to prove it was her?"

"We'll keep digging. Meanwhile, keep your doors locked."

Jayne laughed; she couldn't help herself. She couldn't wrap her head around all the mayhem that had befallen those around her. "Thanks for the tip, officer."

CHAPTER THIRTY-ONE

On Wednesday afternoon, Jayne went with Danny to Buffalo for Dale Diamond's wake. Even though Miss Natalie had known Mr. Diamond for nearly a lifetime, Jayne had decided the crowd at such a somber event might be too much for her, so once again, Hannah was stepping in to keep Miss Natalie company.

When Danny and Jayne arrived, the funeral home parking lot was full. He had to park in the fast-food lot next door. "Mr. Diamond was a popular man," he muttered, turning into the only open spot.

Jayne stared at the white building with two-story pillars and double red doors that screamed funeral home. She found herself traveling back in time to another funeral home at her father's, then her brother's, wakes. Both were police officers. Her father had died from natural causes, and her brother was killed in the line of duty. Both men had been honored in a way befitting a cop. Part of her was envious that as a private investigator, she'd forever be on the outside looking in. Not part of something bigger than herself.

Jayne released a long breath. "I'll pay my respects and we

can go. It shouldn't take long." She immediately regretted the words as soon as they came out of her mouth. She shouldn't be putting a timer on this. This was the end of a man's life.

Once inside the lobby, a black sign with white letters formed the name *Dale Diamond* with an arrow pointing to the right. The crowd from the man's wake spilled into the overflow room. The cloying smell of flowers and something else Jayne tried not to think about reached her nose. When they entered the room that was supposed to resemble a living room, instead of a large-screen TV, an open casket was the focus of attention. Mr. Diamond's daughter Lola, wearing a black dress, greeted each guest with a smile and remarkable composure. When Jayne reached the front of the receiving line, she pulled the woman into an embrace. "I'm sorry, Lola. How are you doing?"

The willowy, thin woman shrugged. Suddenly, her composure cracked and her eyes grew red-rimmed.

"I know, I know. I'm sorry." Jayne reached over and touched Danny's forearm. "This is my friend, Danny Nolan."

"Sorry for your loss," he said.

Lola nodded, then turned her attention back to Jayne. "Have you heard anything? The police insist it was an accident. That he had too much to drink and fell and hit his head." Her lower lip began to quiver. "My dad was an alcoholic who had been sober for twenty years. He wouldn't..."

An alcoholic? This is new information. But did it matter? Plenty of alcoholics had setbacks.

"You were in his room. Did it look like an accident?"

The red fingernail came to mind, but Jayne didn't want to give the woman information that might haunt her if nothing came of it. That would be cruel.

Jayne squeezed Lola's hands. They were cold and trembling. "I'm sure the police are investigating."

"I'm not so sure." Lola's voice was barely a whisper.

Jayne was about to say something when the man behind her took a step forward, as if he were standing in a grocery line and eager to be the next one to check out, rather than expressing his condolences to a grieving daughter. "You have lots of people who want to pay their respects. We'll talk soon, okay?"

Lola nodded, then turned her focus on the impatient man.

Danny guided Jayne toward the door. Once outside in the parking lot, Jayne drew in a deep breath of cold air. "That never gets easier."

Danny wrapped his arm around her shoulders and pulled her close, but he didn't say anything.

"Jayne! Jayne Murphy!" Both Jayne and Danny slowed and turned toward the sound of a woman calling her name.

"Oh, wow, it's Amber," Jayne said, stepping away from Danny.

Amber had on a winter hat tucked low over her ears and the collar of her bright red winter coat flipped up against the cold. She came at Jayne, gesturing with her index finger. She had on leather gloves. "Why did you tell them I was in the room with Dale Diamond?"

Danny held out his hand. "Stand back."

"No, it's okay," Jayne said, somewhat surprised the police had followed up with Amber. Surprised *and* pleased that the Niagara Falls PD had not automatically written Mr. Diamond's death off as an accident as she'd expected. "I found a red acrylic nail under the bed in Mr. Diamond's room. Are you telling me it wasn't yours? I saw you were missing one on Sunday morning." Her heart was thundering in her throat as she studied the woman's face.

"I wasn't in his room." Her eyes appeared black in the shadowy parking lot.

Jayne considered the dark figure going into Mr.

Diamond's room. There was no way of knowing who was on the security video. "Can you prove that you weren't?"

"I had no reason to go his room." Amber was growing more exasperated. Her eyes darted around the parking lot, as if she was trying to figure something out, perhaps an alibi.

Jayne took a step closer. "Not even to convince him to retire because you wanted his job?" She blurted out the words thinking of poor Lola. "Maybe you hadn't meant to kill him, but things got out of hand. He fell, hit his head." She purposely made no mention of the scuff marks on Mr. Diamond's impeccably shined shoes.

"No, no, no. I had no reason to beg for his job. JR had already promised it to me."

"Mr. Diamond had three years on his contract. He wasn't interested in retiring. He was supporting his daughter in New York City."

Amber jerked her head, seemingly taken aback. "No, that can't be true. JR told me that Mr. Diamond was stepping down. That all the travel had become too much for him. It hadn't been announced yet, and I was told to keep it quiet."

Jayne glanced down and saw the woman's hands flexing and unflexing by her side.

"I don't know what he told you, but Mr. Diamond loved that job. He wasn't planning to leave."

Amber's jaw suddenly went slack, then she narrowed her gaze. "I know what must have happened. I know." She cursed under her breath, then seemed to calm herself. "He's lying to us all." Steeling resolve reinforced her conviction. "That jerk," she muttered.

CHAPTER THIRTY-TWO

"Can I get you anything else?" the waitress asked. Jayne suspected the young woman was probably counting the tips she was going to miss because Jayne, Danny, and Amber were occupying a booth but only ordered coffee.

"No, thank you." Jayne waited until the woman was out of hearing range before she spoke. "Okay, Amber, tell me what's going on."

The young woman flattened her hands on the table on either side of her coffee. A coffee that was growing colder by the second. She lifted her watery eyes to the ceiling. "You're going to think poorly of me." Her voice cracked. Amber was either a tremendous actor, or she was genuinely distraught. "He said he loved me. That I was going to be the next face of Superstar Dance Power. We'd travel and be together."

Jayne wanted to state the obvious—that JR was married—but kept it to herself. She needed Amber to keep talking and accusing her of infidelity wasn't going to endear the woman to her.

"It was a perfect plan until JR seemed to get cold feet," Amber continued. "He said we should wait until his youngest was out of high school. That it would look suspicious to his wife if a pretty spokesperson took over for Mr. Diamond. His youngest is ten years old!" Her perfectly groomed eyebrows disappeared behind her long bangs. "I couldn't wait eight years."

Danny lowered his coffee mug. "You're spelling out motive for *you* to kill Dale Diamond."

Amber shook her head, her dangling earrings casting dancing shadows on her neck. "No, no, don't you see? I could never do that." She ran a hand under her nose. "Did you see his poor daughter?" She pressed her trembling lips together. "I didn't want to believe it, but I feel so bad for Lola. That could have been *my* dad."

"What's going on?" Jayne asked, careful to speak in a soothing manner.

"I admired Dale. He was a legend. Sure, I wanted his job, but I wouldn't hurt him. I wanted him to step aside. Retire." She swiped at a tear rolling down her cheek. "I wouldn't wait. I told JR if he didn't make me the master of ceremony for the competition circuit, that I'd go to his wife. We got into a huge fight." She sniffed and her voice grew shaky. "I gave him an ultimatum." She quickly added in a whisper, "I would have never gone to his wife, though. It was an empty threat." She glanced down at her missing fingernail. "I lost an acrylic Friday night and I gave it to JR to hold for me. I wanted to glue it back on. He had pockets," she added, as if it made perfect sense. "Don't you see? He planted my fingernail in Mr. Diamond's room." Her eyes grew wide. "I don't know what happened between the two men, but JR wanted to make sure he wouldn't go down for it." She gritted her teeth.

"That seems pretty convenient," Jayne said, studying the woman's face. She seemed genuinely distraught.

Amber narrowed her gaze. "There's no other explanation. I did *not* hurt Mr. Diamond."

Jayne considered something else she had learned. "Did Mr. Diamond ever make you feel uncomfortable?"

Amber shook her head. "No, Mr. Diamond was always a gentleman to me. However, JR and I..." her voice grew quiet, as if her conscience had suddenly caught up with her "...made some baseless accusations thinking he might retire to avoid ruining his reputation." She cleared her throat and her voice cracked. "It seemed harmless enough."

"Harmless?" Jayne's tone dripped with disdain. "You thought ruining a man's reputation was harmless?"

"I'm an awful person. But I never thought it would go far." Amber swiped at another tear and in that moment, Jayne believed her. Amber's anguish was palpable.

Jayne's heartbeat pounded in her ears as she waited for Amber to continue. "I think JR must have confronted Dale, encouraging him to retire so I wouldn't go to JR's wife about our affair." She scrunched up her face as if the details were too hard to imagine. "Maybe they struggled. Mr. Diamond hit his head." The woman wanted desperately to frame Mr. Diamond's death as an accident, apparently not believing the man she loved—the *cheater* who she loved—could intentionally hurt someone. "That jerk probably dropped my nail in the room to make me look guilty. If it looked like *I* killed Mr. Diamond, *I'd* go to prison and he wouldn't have to hold up his end of the agreement."

"That would take some premeditation," Danny said.

Amber turned her gaze to him. "Do you have a better theory?"

"If your boyfriend framed you, wouldn't it be more likely that you'd go to his wife? Do whatever it took to clear your name?" Danny asked, holding out his hand. "Like now?"

Amber held up her palms. "It was the only thing that makes sense." She laughed bleakly. "Nothing makes sense."

She lifted her chin, steeling herself. "I did *not* hurt Mr. Diamond. Do you believe me?"

Jayne took a sip of her cool coffee. It needed more sugar. Maybe more cream too.

"The Niagara Falls PD were saying it was an accident until you started pushing the theory that *I* killed him, all because you found my red acrylic nail." Amber curled her fingers and studied her nails, now painted in a French manicure. She slowly looked up. "It wasn't me."

Seeing the look of genuine panic in the woman's eyes, Jayne promised her she'd investigate it.

Amber flipped open her expensive-looking purse and dug for something, probably money to pay for the coffee. "I have to pack. I'm flying home right after the funeral tomorrow." She slipped out of the booth. She paused, a faraway look in her eyes. "Don't worry, the police know how to find me once they match the DNA from my fake nail. I'm not running away." She turned and walked away, her sagging posture conveying her defeat.

"What do you think?" Jayne asked Danny.

"It's plausible. But how do we prove it?" He ran a hand across his hair. He looked handsome in his suit from the wake.

"You know, Teddy did some digging. JR's in some serious debt. If he thought he was going to lose Superstar Dance Power, he might do whatever it took to hold onto it. If he felt Amber was going to ruin him if he didn't give her Dale's job, it might be motive enough," Jayne speculated, keeping her voice low.

"Why not hurt Amber? Take her out of the picture."

Jayne twisted her lips, thinking. "Maybe he honestly cares for her. They are having an affair." Jayne rubbed the back of her neck. "Now how do we see what our friend JR was up when Mr. Diamond died?" An idea suddenly hit her. She scrambled out of the booth. "We have to catch up with Amber."

"Amber, hold up!" Jayne ran out into the parking lot, her long winter coat flapping behind her. "Amber!"

The woman stopped at her car, her hand on the door handle. She lifted an eyebrow as if to say, "What?"

"I want to show you a photo. It's not that clear, but..." Jayne dug her phone out of her pocket and clicked a few buttons. Danny caught up and stood next to her, blocking the icy wind. Jayne held out her phone.

Amber looked at the photo, then up at Jayne. "Where was that taken?"

"Do you recognize him?" Jayne pressed.

"It's JR."

"How do you know?"

"That tracksuit. He wears one like it. It's JR," she repeated when she apparently didn't get the right reaction from Jayne. "Where is this?"

"Outside Mr. Diamond's hotel room the night he died."

"This is it. This is the proof." Amber hummed with excitement.

"It's not exactly a smoking gun," Danny said. "The photo is grainy."

Amber bit her lower lip. "What if I agree to talk to JR? Get him to confess. He always lets down his guard around me. I'll wear a wire." She frowned. "Or is that something they only do on TV? Please, I have to do something."

Jayne looked over at Danny, then Amber. "We'd have to organize something with the Niagara Falls police."

"Can it be bright and early tomorrow morning? I want to go home and...I don't know...sleep for a week."

"I'll call Chief Ross," Danny said.

Jayne grabbed her phone out of her purse. "Give me your cell phone number. We'll set it up."

Amber nodded somberly, then smiled and said, "Yes, it's the right thing to do," as if she had to convince herself.

CHAPTER THIRTY-THREE

Jayne stirred her mother's Irish stew, then set the spoon on the ceramic Santa. Jayne should have swapped it out with Valentine's Day, or maybe even St. Patrick's Day so she'd be ahead of the game. "It smells good, Mom."

"Is your friend coming to dinner?" Miss Natalie wrung her hands, the way she had begun to do when she felt a little discombobulated. Jayne didn't want to ask which friend her mother was referring to. Jayne suspected she knew.

"I invited Danny to come by." They had spent a lot of time together this week following the dance competition last weekend. It turned out that Amber Mack had done exactly as she'd promised and caught JR on tape saying he had argued with Dale because he refused to step down. They got into a shoving match, and Dale had whacked his head on the desk in the hotel room, then JR had dragged him into the bathroom. A fall in the bathroom would seem less suspicious. Then, for good measure, he'd left Amber's nail under the bed.

Jayne had listened to the tape. JR confessed in a cocky manner, warning his girlfriend that she had more to lose than he did because solid evidence connected her to the scene of the crime. JR hadn't been counting on his naive girlfriend setting a trap. It had felt so good to get justice for Dale Diamond and answers for his grieving daughter. And on impulse, Jayne had invited Danny to dinner. Like old times.

But Jayne still held the line in the sand. They were nothing more than friends. It was better this way.

The dogs started barking wildly at the front door. Trinket was in her glory with Finn and Melissa's Goldendoodles, the three of them creating a ruckus.

"I think Danny's here now." Of all the guests, he was the only one who would ring the doorbell. On her way to answer it, Jayne scooped up Trinket and patted the other dogs reassuringly on their heads. She pulled open the door and despite herself, her heart fluttered. "Hello, welcome to mayhem."

Danny held out a bouquet of flowers, then pulled them back when he realized she didn't have a free hand to take them. "Thanks for inviting me for dinner. I missed this place." She understood why he hadn't said that he had missed *her*, but it still stung.

"Come on in." Jayne set the dog down and it took a minute for Trinket to gain traction on the smooth tile and join Sean's dogs on the large footstool under the front window where they kept watch over the neighborhood. "We're about to sit down."

Once seated around the table, Melissa and Finn started talking about their upcoming big day. Melissa seemed totally absorbed in all the minutia that went into planning a wedding, and her groom was agreeable to everything. Finn was probably content that his career was going in the right direction. There had been talk of making his interim assignment as chief permanent.

"Mr. Danny," Ava called from across the table, "can you get me more bread?" Jayne's three-year-old niece tended to pick one favorite for each visit. Tonight, it appeared to be Danny.

Jayne pushed back from the table. "I'll get it."

Danny placed his hand on her arm. "No, I got it." He stood and said to no one in particular, "Bread in the kitchen?"

"Yes, on the island," Jayne said.

"Butter, pease!" Ava lisped.

"Butter's in the fridge," Cara, Ava's mother called. "Thank you!"

"So..." Cara lowered her voice, "are you and Danny back on?"

Jayne's face flushed with her entire family watching her. "We're friends," she said, straining her neck, as if to say, "Now be quiet."

Danny returned with a plate of rolls and the butter. "Can I get anyone anything else while I'm up?"

"No, no, sit down, enjoy the meal," Finn said. "You did a great job assisting Niagara Falls PD in solving that murder."

Cara leaned over and placed her hands over her young daughter's ears.

"Come on," Sean said, "can we save that kind of talk for another time?"

Half of Finn's mouth turned up in a grin. "Sorry, I forget sometimes."

"*Jayne* was instrumental in getting the information to solve that case," Danny added, apparently carefully selecting his words.

Finn met Jayne's gaze. "I know. And I should have said as much. My little sister is turning out to be a pretty good private investigator." Jayne wasn't sure if her brother was being sarcastic or sincere, but something on his face told her that her big brother was genuinely proud of her.

"Thanks, Chief Murphy." She found herself squeezing Danny's knee.

Finn laughed, obviously in a good mood.

"Hey, while we're in a celebratory mood," Melissa said. "Jayne, I'd love for you to be one of my bridesmaids."

Jayne pressed her hand to her chest. "I'd love to."

"Well, now that that's settled, let's eat," Miss Natalie said.

While they were finishing up dinner, Jayne's phone started to blow up with texts in the next room. She glanced around the table. Everyone she cared about was sitting with her, so it couldn't be that big of an emergency.

"You wanna get that?" Sean asked.

Jayne rolled her eyes and got up. She snagged her phone from the kitchen counter and glanced at the screen, trying to make sense of what she was seeing: a series of images from inside her house, inside the Greens' house, from the dance competition, and another of Jayne standing in her kitchen taken from the backyard.

A flush of dread washed over her. Jayne grabbed the cord to the blinds and dropped them to cover the back windows.

What does this mean?

Then, as if answering her question, another text popped up, and another and another.

I'm watching you.

I'm going to get you.

There's nowhere to hide.

Jayne returned to the dining room and made eye contact with sweet little Ava. "Danny, may I see you in the kitchen?"

Nausea roiled in her gut as she watched Danny scroll through the photos and the texts. "We need to find Carol Anne—now. She's obviously violated the terms of her release."

"You think it's Carol Anne?" Jayne asked the obvious question.

"She would be my first guess."

Danny strode to the front door and Jayne followed. "Hey, I'm going with you."

The snow on the road leading to Carol Anne's mobile home had grown black from exhaust. It hadn't been cleared like the main arteries, but enough vehicles had traveled it over the past week to make it passable. Jayne's heart was thundering in her ears. Carol Anne was not well and she had turned her fixation on Jayne. Or so it seemed.

And perhaps Jayne's family. That was the worst part.

"The place looks dark," she said, imagining Carol Anne sitting in the old RV without any lights, plotting her revenge.

"Yeah, you want to wait in the truck?" Danny asked.

Jayne shook her head. "I want to look her in the eye when I show her these images." She followed Danny's tracks through the snow and up the stoop. He knocked a few times, but no one answered.

"She's not home!" someone called.

Jayne turned around to find a woman walking her dog. "The girl left yesterday. She was lugging a huge backpack."

Danny pointed to what appeared to be Carol Anne's car buried under six inches of snow. "Her car's here."

"You the police?" she asked.

Jayne was about to say, "No," when Danny confirmed he was.

"She's in trouble, right? She's the one who killed her sister." The large dog the woman was walking tugged on its leash, trying desperately to reach them. "Never understood how she suddenly showed up here after her mom died." The woman put a gloved hand on top of her knit hat, pushing it farther down. "Her mother was a piece of work too."

"You said she's not home?" Jayne pressed, not wanting to gossip about the deceased. "Her car's here."

"That girl hasn't driven that car in ages. Not sure it even runs." The woman jerked her chin toward the trailer. "She cuts through the woods behind here. I can see it perfectly good from my back window. I think she gets one of those Ubers, or whatever."

"Thanks," Danny said.

"I don't think she's coming back," the dog walker said. "Earlier in the week, she had a friend with a truck take away a few boxes and furniture, not that there was anything in that place that isn't saturated with nicotine."

"Do you know this friend?" Jayne asked.

"Me and the neighbors aren't buddy buddy or anything. Just telling you what I seen."

Jayne nodded. "Well, I guess we missed her then." She leaned way over the metal railing on the stoop, and it creaked under her weight. She held her breath hoping it would hold as she peered into the trailer through a window cloudy with years of caked-on dirt. Either Carol Anne and her mother were absolute slobs, or someone had ransacked the place. Danny leaned over her shoulder to see for himself.

He placed his hand on the small of her back and they returned to the truck. He started the engine and cranked the heat. "You okay?"

Jayne stared at the RV. "We have no proof that Carol Anne is behind any of this. Just because she's accused of running her sister off the road and killing her, it doesn't mean she's now harassing me." Even as she spoke the words out loud, she realized how wrong they sounded. "What do we do now?"

"We find Carol Anne. See what she's been up to," Danny said. "Make sure that if it is her behind these photos and the break-in at her father's house, that she doesn't take it any further." He cleared his throat. "I talked to someone where she was under psychiatric observation prior to her release. They refused to tell me anything about her or if she had any friends citing privacy issues."

Jayne leaned back in the seat; her mother's Irish stew unsettled in her belly. "I've had this sinking feeling that someone has been watching me, like at the competition last weekend. Then these photos. We have to find Carol Anne." She turned to Danny. "You know the name of her lawyer?"

"Yes, Robert Park."

Jayne did a quick Google search and gave the man a call. After he confirmed that Carol Anne had been in touch with him and nothing about the terms of her release dictate that she must live in the trailer where she grew up, she hung up in frustration. "That was a dead end."

"At least she's not completely off the radar." Danny reached across and took Jayne's hand and gently squeezed. "You're a great PI. I'm sure you'll find her."

Jayne lifted her gaze to him and smiled. She wished she was as confident as he was right now. "Are you going to leave me up to my own devices?"

He raised an eyebrow and half of his mouth curved into a grin. "Only if you want me to leave you to it."

No, she definitely didn't want him to leave her alone. She returned his smile, then her gaze drifted over to the neighbor watching them from her front stoop. But now was not the place to show him.

Shame, too.

"Well..." Danny put the truck into reverse "...I better get you home before your family wonders where you disappeared to."

Jayne let out a quiet chuckle as she stared at the trailer homes outside the passenger window. The only one who ever really missed her was Miss Natalie who was probably asking Hannah right now where Jayne was. For the millionth time.

The evening unfolded in her mind's eye. Go home. Make sure her mother was settled for the night. Then maybe she and Danny could watch a movie. Or not. She wasn't sure they had fallen back into their familiar routine just yet.

So much indecision.

But one thing she knew for sure, tomorrow she'd get up, stop by Wysocki and Sons' and do some digging. Find out what Carol Anne was really up to. And wait for her next case.

Dear Reader,

Thank you for reading **Corpse de Ballet**. I hope you enjoyed it.

Are you looking for another book by me? I have a bunch listed in the "Also by" section of this book, but can I lead you directly to Grave Danger, one of my romantic suspense novels? Here's the blurb:

She has a secret he'd kill to protect.

Former wild-child Nicole Braun returns home and is forced to accept a job at a funeral home out of reach of the local gossips. But someone knows she's back. Someone who wants her dead. The police chief must look beyond her sordid past to protect her and her son, who has a secret of his own.

Get it on Amazon today!

Thank you and happy reading,
Alison

ALSO BY ALISON STONE

The Thrill of Sweet Suspense Series

(Stand-alone novels that can be read in any order)

Random Acts

Too Close to Home

Critical Diagnosis

Grave Danger

The Art of Deception

Hunters Ridge: Amish Romantic Suspense

Plain Obsession: Book 1

Plain Missing: Book 2

Plain Escape: Book 3

Plain Revenge: Book 4

Plain Survival: Book 5

Plain Inferno: Book 6

Plain Trouble: Book 7

A Jayne Murphy Dance Academy Cozy Mystery

Pointe & Shoot

Final Curtain

Corpse de Ballet

Bargain Boxed Sets

Hunters Ridge Book Bundle (Books 1-3)

The Thrill of Sweet Suspense Book Bundle (Books 1-3)

For a complete list of books visit

Alison Stone's Amazon Author Page

ABOUT THE AUTHOR

Alison Stone is a ***Publishers Weekly bestselling author*** who writes sweet romance, cozy mysteries, and inspirational romantic suspense, some of which contain bonnets and buggies.

Alison often refers to herself as the "accidental Amish author." She decided to try her hand at the genre after an editor put a call out for more Amish romantic suspense. Intrigued—and who doesn't love the movie *Witness* with Harrison Ford?—Alison dug into research, including visits to the Amish communities in Western New York where she lives. This sparked numerous story ideas, the first leading to her debut novel with Harlequin Love Inspired Suspense. Four subsequent Love Inspired Suspense titles went on to earn ***RT magazine's TOP PICK!*** designation, their highest ranking.

When Alison's not plotting ways to bring mayhem to Amish communities, she's writing romantic suspense with a more modern setting, sweet romances, and cozy mysteries. In order to meet her deadlines, she has to block the internet and hide her smartphone.

Married and the mother of four (almost) grown kids, Alison lives in the suburbs of Buffalo where the summers are gorgeous and the winters are perfect for curling up with a book—or writing one.

Be the first to learn about new books, giveaways and deals in Alison's newsletter. Sign up at AlisonStone.com.
Connect with Alison Stone online:
www.AlisonStone.com
Alison@AlisonStone.com

Made in the USA
Las Vegas, NV
25 October 2022